# AWA AND THE DREAMREALM

## DREAMWEAVERS BOOK 1

### ISA PEARL RITCHIE

TE RĀ

First published 2019

© Isa Pearl Ritchie 2019

ISBN 978-0-473-49574-9

A catalogue record for this book is available from the National
Library of New Zealand

TE RĀ AROHA PRESS

*For Tesla, Kaurangaihi, Ngahere, Charlotte, Vidthia,*
*Maddie, Max and James...*
*...and all the children who dream of other worlds*

We are creatures of words. We are creatures of imagination. We live on the edges of dreams and the margins of thought. We live in the whisper of the page.

– *Whiti Hereaka, Pūrākau*

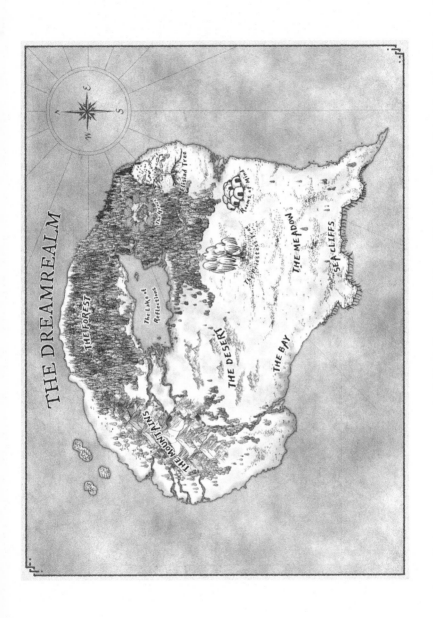

# PROLOGUE

$\mathcal{I}$ watched her slide through the holographic tunnel. She landed silently in the dark room, like a bright puddle of radiance at the foot of the bed. She was toddler-sized, but adult-shaped and glowing. She looked as if she was made of dazzling peach-coloured light.

She floated up, sending light and shadows swimming around the room. She looked down at the girl sleeping in the bed.

"It's a small one," the glowing creature said to herself, "…must be a young one."

She moved closer, illuminating the girl's face and chin-length hair, dark and messy, spread across her pillow. The girl's skin was light brown, and little freckles were clustered across her nose and cheeks, a bit like mine…

That was when it hit me.

*It IS me – this is my face!*

She was looking at me, sleeping: it was my bed, my bedroom.

*I must be dreaming.*

The creature leaned down and whispered in my ear: "A snowstorm... a friendly polar bear... beware the gate-keepers."

The vibrant images swam through my mind, as I jumped back into my body.

My eyes flew open to find I was still in the unusual dream I was having.

"Hello?" I said to the little glowing creature in front of me.

She squeaked like the sound of a dog toy. Her mouth opened so wide in surprise it looked like a little "o."

"Are you... real?" I asked.

"You – you can see me?"

"Of course," I said.

She stared at me as if I was the most unbelievable thing she had ever witnessed.

"What's your name?" I asked her. "If you even have one."

"I'm Veila," she said.

"Hi Veila, I'm Awa," I replied.


And that was how I met Veila... but I'm getting ahead of myself. The story really began a couple of weeks earlier, the night after we moved.

 t wasn't until I got to the very last box that I found them – my special toys. I know I'm too old for soft toys, but these ones were important, and I had been looking for them the whole time I was unpacking the zillions of boxes from the old house, or as Mum would say: cluttering up my room with all this stuff I don't really need! She was totally wrong about that, but it didn't help that my new room in the apartment was so small compared to the old house. I sighed, just thinking about it made me want to be back there.

I arranged them carefully at the foot of my bed: my favourite bunny Bobo, next to Squiddy the purple squid and my koala, Sir George Stanfordshire the Third (Stan for short).

I had carried them around with me wherever I went as a kid, especially Bobo, who was showing his age. Something about his gentle smile always made me feel better. I lay across my bed, hugging him, wishing everything could go back to the way it was before. Things used to be brighter, lighter… now I just felt so heavy and tired. I yawned and closed my eyes.

*Bluey-white light shone from behind a door. I raised my hand to push it open, revealing stars – thousands and millions of stars!*

I opened my eyes, coming back into my bedroom and away from the floating feeling of the dream I was just having.

The sky looked darker outside. I must have slept through dinner time and I was starving.

Mum's bedroom light was on.

"There's a plate of lasagne for you in the fridge," she called out as I passed.

*It must be late.*

I had never looked out of these windows at night before. Outside, I could see thousands of lights, some far in the distance, some near. It was quite a pretty view, but even more interesting were the apartments across the road.

I could see into them. A few people were moving between rooms, sitting or standing. Art hung on the walls next to bookshelves and furniture. The effect of being far away made them seem like dollhouses. It was satisfying to look at.

I realised that if I turned the light on they would be able to see me too, so I left it off. I took the plate from the fridge and warmed the cold lasagne in the microwave. When it was ready, I poured hot sauce all over it and carried it over to the couch. I sat there, in the dark, eating and watching the apartments.

It wasn't the same as being in the old house, but it wasn't bad.

"What are you doing out here in the dark?" Mum asked, coming into the room.

"Don't turn the light on! Look!" I pointed out the window.

Mum came over and sat down next to me. "I like that apartment – with all the bookshelves," she said.

"We should get lots of bookshelves too," I replied.

"That sounds like a good plan."

I drifted off to sleep that night thinking about bookshelves and all the great books we could get to fill them with.

Bluey-white light shone from behind a door. I raised my hand to push it open, revealing millions of stars! They swirled in shades of blue, purple and gold.

I felt so floaty and light, as if I was high up, far away from all my troubles.

A platform with a magnificent chalice appeared in front of me. A small white light sparked at the top, as if it knew I was there. It started pouring over like liquid, sending waves of stars flooding out around the sides. I needed to touch that light, whatever it was. I reached forward until the tip of my index finger touched the stars – my whole body lit up with pure joy.

"Awa!"

I opened my eyes, "No!"

I turned over, away from Mum's voice, trying to get back there – to the room with the walls made of stars. I wanted to hold onto the feeling, but it was slipping away.

*... the best feeling ever!*

"Awa! Get up! Get Dressed!"

"Mum!" I moaned.

"You're going to be late for your first day!"

By the time I was up and breakfasted and dressed and ready and in the car, I'd almost forgotten the dream.

"Awa!" Mum looked across at me grumpily from the driver's seat, "Did I tell you that you could paint your nails?"

I looked down at my hand to see the tip of my index finger sparkling like purple stars. *"No way!"* I whispered.

*I was dreaming – but I'm definitely awake now.*

As we drove through the busy streets, I wondered, *could it have been real?*

"Do you want me to walk you in?" Mum asked, jolting me back to reality. We were parked outside the school.

"No!" I blushed at the embarrassment of having my mother, in her really awkward looking red work jacket with the shoulder pads, walking me into school on my first day.

"Okay – if you're sure."

Mum patted me on the shoulder. She was probably just trying to reassure herself that this was okay – that moving to the city was okay, that everything was fine after the divorce – when really it was horrible. I didn't want to think about it. I gritted my teeth and opened the car door. I stepped out into the icy Wellington wind.

"Just go to the office, honey – they will help you find your classroom, okay?"

*I know Mum, I'm not a baby, I'm almost thirteen for crying out loud!*

I closed the door, distracted by the swarm of other kids, who all seemed to be wearing 'nice' clothes – not my style at all!

They looked like something out of a fashion magazine – what Mum would call "business casual."

I looked down at my ripped jeans and stripy long sleeve top.

*This is not good... this is not a good sign.*

I brushed my hair over my face with my fingers, trying to hide. Another sound interrupted the chatter of kids. The car window was being wound down. Mum started to talk again.

*Don't make this worse!*

I pulled my bag on and ran across the road towards the school entrance, a big white archway with the words "Magnolia Heights Intermediate" across the top.

There was no uniform, so why did the kids all look like they were wearing the same thing? And why were they all looking at me like I was some kind of freak?

My new classroom was already crowded when I got there. Some kids stood by the window, chatting, others sat at their desks; they all seemed to stare at me. The teacher, who I had been told was called Mr Jasper, looked up from his desk as I walked in.

"You must be Awa," he said. "Take a seat, we're about to start."

I sat at the nearest desk, trying to avoid the stares of the other students. The bell rang, and the kids started rushing around.

"That's my desk!" said a tall girl with blonde hair. "Move!"

I felt my stomach tighten again.

Not now, the last thing I need is a panic attack.

The classroom around me started fading to grey. I had already left it too long to respond.

I looked down at my hands on the desk in front of me, at purple sparkles still glimmering on my fingernail. I tried to remember the dream – to get back to that good feeling.

"What's wrong with you?" the girl said. "It's my desk, and I said move!"

"Give it a rest Felicity," Mr Jasper said. "The desks belong to the school, and no one can claim them as their own."

"But Mr Jasper," Felicity said, "She's breaking the rules – look, she's wearing nail polish."

I tried to hide my hands.

"Awa is new, Felicity," Mr Jasper said, turning to me. "There is a no make-up rule at this school," he said, with a stern voice.

There was nothing I could say. No one was going to believe me anyway. I just nodded and tried to breathe.

He turned to the class. "Take a seat, kids!" he called.

"You're going to regret this," Felicity said, quietly so that only I could hear. "And by the way – where did you get those clothes? You look like you just crawled out of a gutter."

I didn't respond. I just kept looking down at the desk until she left me alone.

"Good morning, everyone. This is Awa, our newest member," Mr Jasper said, gesturing towards me. "Please show her what an awesome school this is by being kind." Some of the kids snickered; I blushed.

"Who would like to volunteer to show her around?"

Several hands shot up.

"Thanks, Ella," Mr Jasper said. I turned to see a girl with a light brown bob cut a few desks over wearing a yellow cardigan. The girl smiled, and I felt relieved. At least there was one nice kid at this school.

Ella showed me around the school and shared her mandarin with me as we walked. The school was painted in bright colours, and everything seemed a lot newer than my old school.

I guess that's what a school in a neighbourhood full of wealthy 'professionals' looks like.

I knew Mum had chosen this school, even though it was expensive because she thought it would be good for my education – which is obviously a huge waste of money because I'm not one of those kids who's ever going to be good at school work. She also chose it because it's close to the law firm where she had just gotten her first proper lawyer job, and Dad's accountancy office. Most of the office buildings were not too far away, close to Parliament and the Beehive, which is that strangely-shaped building where the Prime Minister works.

"That's pretty much the whole school," Ella said. She lifted her cardigan sleeve and glanced at a teddy-bear watch, then quickly hid it under her cuff again.

She looked up at me to see if I was judging her, but I just smiled.

"Morning break is about to end," she said. Just then the bell rang for us to go back to class.

It felt like a long day. Mum talked in the car on the way home, but I barely listened. I was too tired.

We got back to the apartment. I still wasn't used to it, the big concrete walls were so different from the wooden house I grew up in, and that I missed so much. It wasn't that the building was that bad. If I didn't have to live there, I might have admired the curved shape of it, the patterns on the outside painted in pastels.

I went straight to my room, dropping my bag on the floor and getting into bed.

Mum poked her head around the door.

"Are you okay, honey?"

"Leave me alone!" I groaned. "I'm tired."

"Okay, let me know if you need anything."

I just wanted everything to go back to the way it was before the divorce. I wanted my two-storied house back with its big garden. I wanted my friends to be around all the time, but it seemed like they had less and less time for me since the move, even my best friend, Melody. The tears started trickling down my cheeks and I did nothing to stop them. Eventually, I fell into a light sleep.

# CHAPTER TWO

*I* didn't want to get out of bed the next morning. I lay there, looking at the fingernail that had been so weirdly purple and glittery the day before. It still looked a bit shimmery. Something told me I'd had more strange dreams, even though I couldn't remember them.

The thing is, I used to know who I was – before everything changed. I was the kid who took my toy bunny Bobo everywhere I went, who refused to wear shoes and climbed all the trees in the garden, who collected rocks and shells. I was happy, but now... It all seemed so far away.

My second day at school was just as awkward as the first. It was even worse in some ways because Ella was sick and so I had no one to hang out with. I wasn't even sure if she wanted to be my friend or if she was just being nice to me because Mr Jasper asked her to show me around.

As I packed up my books at morning break, Felicity strutted over to me again.

"I hope you enjoyed sitting at *my* desk," she said. I ignored her, but made a note never to sit there again; it wasn't worth it!

"Awa is a *weird* name," Felicity continued. "Where are you even from?"

I gritted my teeth at Felicity pronouncing my name wrong, making the "A" sound funny, instead of the calm even "ah-wah" that it was supposed to be.

I stayed silent. At my old school, there were lots of kids from all kinds of backgrounds – but almost everyone here was white.

"I'm from New Zealand, just like you," I said, through gritted teeth.

"You look a bit Asian," Felicity said, sneering, "but Awa is a *Māori* name, isn't it?"

I didn't respond again. I hated the way she said Māori. Mum always said you could tell if someone is racist by the way they pronounce it.

I just had to get past Felicity and out of the classroom, and then I would be free of the awful feeling in my stomach– at least for a little while.

"You're a bit of a mongrel, aren't you?" Felicity said as I pushed past her.

My gut tightened in disgust, but I didn't say a word.

I got home feeling just as tired as when I woke up. I dropped my school bag on the ground and kicked off my shoes. A familiar tune was coming from my bag.

*My phone!*

I quickly grabbed it from underneath my lunchbox.

*Melody calling*, it said.

"Hello?" I looked into the tiny screen at my best friend's face. It was such a relief to see her.

"Awa!" Melody squealed. "So good to see you!"

"You too!" I said. I had been wondering if I would ever hear from my old friends again.

"How's Wellington? What's it like living in the city? Do you love it?"

"It's… okay, I guess," I lied.

"I miss you so much – and there's so much to tell you about school and – oh – so much gossip!"

"Tell me everything," I said. I wasn't really feeling in the mood for gossip, I just wanted to be connected to my old life.

"I will, but first – oh my gosh – do you know what's happened to your house?"

"What?"

My heart pounded.

"It's gone!"

"Gone?"

"Just gone. They must have busted it down overnight."

Something broke inside me.

It was only a few months since the house was sold. I had gone up North to stay with Nannie and my great-aunt Rosetta while Mum looked for a new place to live. I didn't realise I would never see it again.

"It was so quick. All the trees are gone now too," Melody continued. "It's just like a blank section where your house used to be."

I closed my eyes against the feelings.

"Are you okay?"

"I just remembered something," I said, my voice low, but not crying; definitely not crying. "I've got to go. I'll call you back when I have the chance – say hi to everyone from me."

"Wait!" said Melody.

I hung up and threw myself across the bed so that I could cry properly, in peace. I sobbed into the pillows, crying for the house... my house. I pictured it, with the stained glass, the green veranda, and matching green around the windows. I always thought it looked like something out of a fairy-tale. It was perfect, *and now it's gone.*

I was sitting in the lounge when I heard Mum's key in the lock, and the sound of her walking down the hallway.

"Did you *know?*" I asked, before she had even entered the room.

"Hello, nice to see you too," Mum responded before she saw the look on my face. "Know what, honey?"

"Know what would happen to our house!"

"What do you mean?"

"Melody called – it's gone."

"Oh," Mum said. "How?"

"I guess they demolished it – and all the trees too – it's like we were never there – like our whole lives never existed at all!"

Tears were running down my cheeks, and my voice was cracking, but I didn't care.

"That's a bit of a shock," Mum said, "but it's just a house, honey, it's not our lives."

"It's not just a house!" I sobbed. "It's a home – it *was*... I grew up there. Don't you even care about that?"

"Awa," Mum said, but I had already gotten up.

I stormed down the hallway, slammed my door closed, and threw myself on my bed. *I'll call Dad; maybe he will care.*

"Awa – hi – look, I'm just in a meeting at the moment – I'll call you back, okay."

He hung up the phone. Blinking back more tears, I typed Dad a message instead:

Hi Dad, I just wanted to tell you that our house –
the one we used to live in – is gone now. It's just
gone. There's nothing left. Anyway, I hope you're
having a good meeting. Bye.

*How could this happen?* My parents didn't even care. Maybe no one cared but me. I cried until I was too tired to cry anymore, and then I drifted off to sleep with heavy eyes.

I felt the sensations under-foot: the ground I knew so well, tree roots in the dry summer grass. The scent of my Nannie's freshly baked rēwana bread drifted through the air. Something lit up inside me – like I'd stumbled back into a memory of the last time I'd felt properly happy. I was walking on the lawn of my old house, under the old redwood, past the magnolia tree. I looked up towards the house with its familiar green edging.

I wanted to explode into celebration, *Melody was wrong!*

Then, as the house blurred and shifted in front of me, I realised I couldn't possibly be there. My excitement sank and swirled into a dark heavy feeling.

*You're not real anymore,* I thought, looking up at the house.

*I must be dreaming, but it feels like I'm awake... how strange.*

Everything seemed to slide into itself. The view around me faded at the edges. I saw movement and looked up at the house again. Someone was at the window, a boy with a pale face, looking out. *The ghost of the house,* the thought came. A chill ran down my spine. I turned to run, terrified that the ghost would follow me, would haunt me, I woke up to a buzzing sound.

My phone was ringing. *Dad,* the screen read.

"Hello?" I said, my voice was croaky with sleep.

I wondered why my dad was calling in the night

before I realised I must have fallen asleep in the afternoon again.

"Awa! I'm sorry, did I wake you?" he asked. "It's only eight-thirty."

"It's okay," I said. "I was just resting. School has been busy, and I was tired."

"Oh," Dad replied, "look, I just wanted to say I'm sorry about before. I've been so busy with work, and I'm also sorry I haven't seen you lately."

"It's okay, Dad," I said, with that good feeling I get when Dad pays attention to me, like warm sunshine.

"And I'm sorry about the house too," said Dad. "It's so sad they did that."

"Yeah," I said, but there wasn't much else I could say.

"I mean," Dad's voice continued although I had pulled away from the phone, "once we sold it, we had no control, and we had to sell, you know, because of the divorce."

I held back the tears that kept trying to burst out.

"I know."

"Anyway, let's hang out soon. How about we go for pizza next week?"

"Sounds good," I said, feeling the warmth fade and the longing come back.

"I'll let you go, but I just want to say I love you and I care about you, sweetie."

"I love you too, Dad."

I dropped the phone onto my bed and rolled over. At least Dad understood.

I picked up the book I'd found in the school library. It was really good – about this kid whose family had to move to the other side of the world to get away from a nasty criminal. I even read while eating dinner – fried rice with extra chili sauce. I forgot all about the creepy dream I'd had until Mum told me it was bedtime.

As soon as I was alone in my room, getting my pyjamas on, the feeling came back, like I was being watched.

I left the light on and got into bed.

"Time for lights out, sweetie," Mum said, leaning against the door frame. She looked tired.

"I'm just gonna sleep with it on tonight."

Mum sighed. "Not this again, Awa."

"Come on, Mum. I won't be able to sleep otherwise. I had a nightmare about the house, and there was this creepy kid staring at me through the window."

"You only just found out about the house."

"It was this afternoon – I had a nap."

"Really?" Mum said I could tell she didn't believe me.

"Yes – really!"

"Why do you keep falling asleep in the afternoon?" Mum asked.

"I'm tired?!"

Mum sighed again. She came in and sat down on my bed.

"Look, honey. I know all this change has been hard on you, and not seeing your dad much…"

"I see him enough," I said, even though it was true that I hadn't actually seen him for a while.

"Is there anything I can do, to make things easier?"

"Just let me sleep with the light on, okay?"

"Okay – but don't make a habit of it," Mum said. "It's not good for your sleep."

She hugged me and left the door open, and the hallway light on too, just how I like it.

# CHAPTER THREE

It happened over and over again. I dreamed about the old house every single night since I'd heard the news that it was gone. It was the house I had grown up in. I knew every inch of it, and now my dreams were tracing it.

*Walking down the hallway...*

*Standing in the kitchen...*

*Going from room to room...*

I opened the door. I was staring into the dark hallway of my old house. Light flickered down the walls just as a shiver ran down my spine. *I'm not supposed to be here.*

The shadows moved and shifted around me as I seemed to glide through the house.

I got to the kitchen; bright light lit up the old yellow linoleum floor and the orange cupboards with their peeling paint. That's when I saw it. It was dark green and slithering on the floor:

*A huge snake!*

It lifted its head and hissed at me. I ran to the back door, and out into the night.

It felt unsafe out there too. The land around me looked haunted and empty except for the forest. There was no forest here before. *I must be dreaming.* I turned back to see the house had morphed into an old church.

There was movement out of the corner of my vision:

*The snake!*

It was even bigger, and it was coming right towards me.

*No!* I screamed and ran into the dark forest. I could hear the twigs cracking under its weight and the hissing as it followed me, closer and closer, growing larger and larger.

All I could do was run!

I woke up, my heart racing from the nightmare. I rolled over in my bed and pulled the covers up over my head, wrapping myself in a ball.

*It's okay,* I tried to reassure myself, *it's just a dream,* but dreams meant something different now. A sparkle was still just visible on my index finger even though it had almost completely faded. *If dreams are real – I don't want anything to do with them!*

The snake dream kept coming back to my mind at school over the next few days. It felt so real!

I wondered whether there was something wrong with my brain, or whether there really was something after me: something evil. I mostly kept to myself at school because I didn't feel very social. I hung out in the library at lunchtimes and looked up everything I could find about dreams and snakes and demons... and I made myself feel even worse!

School hadn't gotten much better. I tried to avoid Felicity, but I did notice her looking at me and giggling with some of her friends, probably calling me horrible names behind my back.

It was lunchtime when I saw Ella again.

"Felicity's awful, isn't she?" Ella said.

I nodded. I didn't know what else to say. As we walked out into the courtyard and into the sunshine, the tightness lifted. I sighed.

"What's *wrong* with her?" I asked Ella.

"That's a good question – she's always been like that, as far as I can remember."

"I didn't do anything to her except accidentally sit in her seat. What does she have against me?"

"That's just Felicity, Ella said. "She's jealous of you because you're new, so you get more attention from the teachers and because you're cool.

"I find that very hard to believe. I said I've never once been cool in my entire life."

"You are!" Ella insisted. "You dress differently, and you're... I don't know... you're your own person – you're not trying to be like everyone else."

"Maybe it's more that she's racist," I said.

"Maybe," Ella replied. "I never really noticed."

Later that day Ella asked, "Do you want to come over next weekend for a sleepover?"

I didn't know what to say. The school bell had just rung, and I was packing up my bag. I liked Ella, but what if I talked in my sleep when I was dreaming – or worse, what if I have another snake nightmare and scream?

"I'll ask my mum," I said, smiling, but deep down I was worried.

I walked out of the school gates into a gust of typical Wellington wind. There was too much to think about.

That was when I saw it: the snake tattoo. It was green and looked as if it was glistening, and it was on the arm of a big hulking man, standing outside the school gates with a black t-shirt and ripped jeans.

I stared. The snake looked just like the one from my nightmares! I stood, stock-still, staring at the man. A tingle of fear ran up my spine.

It was so weird – the way things from my dreams were turning up in real life. I looked at the man's face, and he smiled at me. I flinched and began walking, quickly away, trying my best not to run. *Running shows them you're afraid.*

I continued walking as quickly as I could until I

turned a corner, out of sight. I stopped panting. *He must be evil... he must be dangerous.*

I tried to think of something else – to push the image of the man and the snake out of my mind, but it kept coming back. *What was he even doing outside my school?* I wondered. A hundred paranoid thoughts rushed through my head. *Maybe he's after me,* I checked behind me, but no one was there. I looked suspiciously into the passing cars, but the man wasn't in any of them. I ran home, against the wind, keeping a constant watch on everything and everyone around me.

I slammed the door behind me as soon as I got home. Mum came down the hallway.

"Awa, what's wrong?"

I was still catching my breath.

"Nothing," I lied, but I could tell from her look that Mum didn't believe me.

"It doesn't seem like nothing," Mum said. "You look like you've seen a ghost." She pulled me into a hug.

"I *feel* like I have!" I said.

I didn't know how much to tell her. I told her about the man with the snake tattoo, but that didn't make sense without telling her about the dream too. Once I started talking, everything just came out – the dreams about the old house, the strange thing with the starry room, and my fingernail.

"It's like my dreams are real," I said.

"Awa," Mum said. She looked concerned. "Let's have a hot chocolate."

I sat down, waiting for my heartbeat to slow back to

normal. Mum moved slowly around the kitchen, making hot drinks. She had a worried look, and I wondered if I had made a mistake in telling her. It felt so good to tell someone, but it seemed crazy even as I was telling it to Mum.

She sat down with me on the couch, passing me my hot chocolate that was the perfect temperature to drink.

"Look, honey…" Mum started.

"I know – it sounds crazy…" I said. "Just please believe me!"

"Awa," Mum said. "How can I…" her voice trailed off.

We sat in silence for a moment.

"I know things have been hard lately with the move and the divorce and the new school."

"It's not that!" I said, my voice rising in anger. Why couldn't she just trust me?

"You've been having trouble with anxiety."

"Mum – I've had anxiety since before the divorce."

"Yes, that's exactly what I want to talk to you about, honey." She lowered her eyes. "You won't remember this, because you were a baby, but…"

"What?"

"It's hard to explain," Mum said, and I could see tears in the corners of her eyes, "but I think the anxiety might have started when you were very young. It was… a difficult birth. You were born too early."

"I know I was a prem baby, Mum."

"Yes, but you don't know how... how all that affected me."

"What do you mean?" I asked. I looked at Mum's face where a tear had started to trickle down her cheek. She brushed it away.

"I wasn't well for quite a while after you were born, which made it really hard for me to take care of you. I spent a lot of time resting in bed and feeling awful. I felt so guilty, Awa. I didn't know what to do. I think that difficult time was what caused you to be an anxious child."

"Maybe it did," I said. "But that's not the same as my dreams becoming real." I put my cup down on the coffee table and got up. It didn't seem like she was listening to me at all!

"Look, honey, maybe there is no connection." Mum said, her eyes had a pleading look. "But I think we should do something about the anxiety."

"What do you mean?" I asked.

"I talked to your father about you being anxious at school. He thinks it might help if you see a therapist that specialises in this kind of thing."

"What?"

"I didn't agree with him," Mum said. "I thought he was jumping to extremes again, but now..."

"Now you think there's something wrong with my brain!" I yelled.

*So that's what I get for telling people the truth!* I stormed to my room. *I'm never doing that again!*

# CHAPTER FOUR

*I* was looking forward to the weekend because Melody, my best friend from my old school, was coming over for a sleepover. I hadn't seen her for ages.

I got home from school on Friday afternoon and tidied my room before Melody arrived. At 5, I got a message saying she was running late — *typical Melody.* I finally heard the apartment buzzer at 6 and ran to let her in.

"Hey!" I called as she came through the door, her strawberry blonde curls bouncing around her shoulders.

"Awa!" Melody hugged me. "So good to see you!"

She looked around, "Hi Vivian!" she called to my mother, who was in the kitchen, making dinner.

"Hi, Melody, welcome to our new home," Mum said.

"It's great here," Melody said. "I mean, it's small, but it's so close to town."

"It is a bit of a change," Mum said.

I dragged Melody away before she got stuck into conversation with my mother. They got along way too well.

We hung out in my room. I felt self-conscious about how messy it was with all my stuff from my old house packed into a smaller space. Melody didn't seem to mind.

We watched some online videos by Valerie Sparkles and Todd Brainstorm.

"Can we order pizza?" Melody asked. "I'm starving."

"Mum's making Bolognese," I said. I didn't want to tell her that I hated asking Mum to spend money, especially at the moment, because she seemed so stressed about it.

"Pizza is better," Melody said, "but I do like spaghetti."

"You like Mum's cooking too," I reminded her.

"Very true," she said, then she changed the conversation. "Hey... so what's the gossip?"

"What gossip?" I asked.

"New school... what's it like?"

"It's... it's fine," I lied.

"It doesn't sound fine," Melody said.

"Well, it's just... I don't know anyone yet; I don't really have proper friends. I mean, I've known you since kindergarten, and I knew enough about people at our old school to know who I wanted to be friends with, but I just don't know…"

"You'll make friends," Melody assured me. "How about boys?"

"What?"

"Cute boys – tell me!"

"Oh, uhh… I don't know," I said.

"Awa!"

"What?"

"I need details!"

"I said, I don't know."

Melody threw herself down on the bed, "You are of no use to me!" she yelled into a pillow. I laughed. She turned around, "I need you to keep records of all the cute boys and their phone numbers – get their phone numbers!"

"I'm not going to do that, Melly."

Melody glared, in that joking way that was one of her usual expressions. Mum brought us plates of hot, steamy spaghetti Bolognese which she said we had to eat at my desk. It was delicious, and Melody forgot all about the pizza idea, *thank goodness*.

It took us a while to choose a movie. Eventually, we settled on a teen drama that had recently come out, but Melody had watched it before and kept interrupting to tell me about *her* latest dramas.

"So Julie won't even talk to me now," she said.

"Should we pause the movie?" I asked, turning towards her.

"No, why would we do that?" Melody replied; she gave me a blank look.

"because you keep talking," I said.

"This is not even an interesting part," Melody insisted. "Julie said that I stopped talking to her first."

"Really?"

"Yes, and it was about Mike Bradley,"

"Who?"

"Mike – who I have been crushing on for months!" Melody said. "Keep up!"

I paused the movie.

"Look," I said. "Either we watch, or we talk because I can't really do both."

"Awa!" Melody said, clearly frustrated.

"What?"

"I don't think you really want to watch this movie, and I don't think you really want to listen to me, either," Melody was serious this time.

"You're probably right," I admitted.

"What's going on with you?" she asked.

"I don't think you'd believe me if I told you," I said, looking up at my poster of Valerie Sparkles my favourite online video star. I'd never noticed before that her pink and purple hair was surrounded by swirls of stars, suspiciously like the ones in my dream.

"Tell me!" Melody insisted.

"Okay," I told her a bit about the dreams I had been having, and how real they were.

"They're just nightmares, Awa," Melody said.

"Not all of them are scary," I said. "And they're not

31

just dreams; there was that thing with my fingernail – it sparkled for days!"

"That is pretty weird," Melody admitted, "but it's probably just a coincidence… like you painted your nail with some kind of sparkly paint and forgot about it, and then your brain made up the dream because of the paint…"

"I don't think so," I said. "I only have bright green nail polish."

"It sounds to me like you have some issues with your old house being destroyed, and you need to get over it."

"Melody!" It was my turn to throw myself down on the bed.

"We should talk about it," she insisted.

"No! I don't want to."

"Awa!"

"Is everything alright in here?" Mum popped her head around the door, and I realised that everything wasn't alright, my heart was racing; the icy feeling was closing in. The room around me was going grey.

"Fine," I called out, to Mum. "We're fine, leave us alone."

I pulled a pillow over my head.

"We're not fine, are we?" Melody said.

I shook my head.

"You've changed," said Melody. "You used to be fun, and now you just want to talk about dreams. They're just dreams, Awa."

"Maybe it's just not fun anymore because it's not all about you and your dramas," I said.

I put the movie back on, and turned up the volume, even though I could barely pay attention to it.

My mind raced over all kinds of anxious thoughts all night, even after Melody fell asleep.

*Melody is my best friend. Melody **was** my best friend. We have nothing in common. She is so pushy. All she cares about is boys and school drama... I don't even know what I care about anymore. I have no real friends. **No friends**. I'm all alone.*

I could barely sleep all night, which had the bonus of meaning no nightmares, but the awful feelings stayed with me, even after Melody went home.

I was so exhausted the next night that I went to sleep super early. That was the night I met Veila.

# CHAPTER FIVE

*S*he slid down through the tunnel of light. I saw the peach coloured glow as she landed silently at the foot of the bed. That was when I noticed how small she was: about the size of a toddler, but shaped more like an adult and glowing as if she was made of light. She floated up and looked down at the girl sleeping in the bed.

"It's a small one," the glowing creature said to herself. "Must be a young one – the young humans are usually more open."

She moved closer so that her light illuminated the girl's face.

I took a closer look too.

*What's so special about this girl?*

Her chin-length hair spread, dark and messy, across her pillow; her skin looked light brown and there was a cluster of little freckles across her nose and cheeks, a bit like mine...

That was when it hit me.

*It IS me – this is my face!*

She was looking at me: it was my bed, my bedroom. It was me asleep in bed.

*I must be dreaming.*

The peachy coloured creature leaned down and whispered in my ear: "A snowstorm… a friendly polar bear. Beware the gate-keepers," she said, as if they were lines she'd memorised.

The images she whispered swam through my mind, as I jumped back into my body.

"Hmph… what does any of that even mean?" she muttered to herself.

My eyes opened to find that I was still in the strange dream I was having.

"Wow!" the single syllable fell out of her mouth.

"Hello?" I said to the strange little glowing creature in front of me.

She squeaked like a dog toy. Her mouth was open so wide in surprise it looked like a little "o."

"Are you… real?" I asked.

"You… you can see me?" She looked at me in astonishment.

"Of course," I said. "What are you made of?" I reached out my hand, "light?"

My fingers tingled as they got close to her. She moved away from me.

"Are you some kind of fairy?" I asked squinting at her, but she moved so quickly it was hard to see the details.

"Fairy? Hah. No," she said, flipping around in the air, giggling.

"Then… what?"

"I'm a dreamcharmer."

She paused, mid-air beaming at me, the light from her glow continued to flicker around the walls even while she stayed still in the air, lighting up my messy room.

"A *what*?!"

"I kind of… give you ideas for your dreams."

"And what's the point of that?" I asked.

But she didn't answer; she just stared at me as if I was the most unbelievable thing she had ever seen.

"What's your name?" I asked her. "If you even have one."

"I'm Veila," she said.

"Hi Veila, I'm Awa," I replied.

"I've heard stories about ones like you," she said, resting her tiny chin against her hands, "…but never – I didn't really believe… you can see me?"

She darted around the room again as if to check to see if my eyes followed her.

"Of course I can," I said.

I did not enjoy being teased, even it is was by a beautiful glowing peachy-coloured creature.

"And what do you mean 'ones like me'?"

"Sensitives," Veila explained.

"I am not!" I said stubbornly, but tears started to well up at the bottom of my eyes.

"You – well, most of you humans… can't see us at all. It's really very special," Veila said.

"Not humans – then… animals can see you?"

"Cats usually, sometimes birds, spiders, lizards… a few other things, you know..."

"You look like a fairy, but all light and no wings – where do you come from?"

"Well, not here… but, outside of here."

I didn't know what she was talking about, but I had the feeling she didn't mean next door or the next town over… more like the next world over.

"And… why?" I tried to ask again, but it was too late, a cascade of bells sounded from somewhere above. Veila whispered goodbye, as the light began to shine more brightly around her. As the light faded, I realised I was alone again in my dark bedroom.

I pinched myself. *Definitely awake.*

*What the hell was that all about?*

I got to school the next day in a bit of a daze, not sure what was real or imagined anymore. As soon as I saw Felicity, I forgot all about the strange dream creature from the night before. She glared at me as I arrived in class, a few minutes early.

"Loser," she said, not loud enough for anyone else to hear. "Freak." She made her voice even quieter. "Mongrel."

I didn't reply, but the words stung, especially after the fight I had with Melody in the weekend.

Felicity blocked my path as I tried to cross the room.

"I see you're still dressing like a gutter freak," she said. I looked down. I was wearing denim shorts over my purple tights and my jellyfish t-shirt.

*There's nothing wrong with me,* I told myself. *It's Felicity that has the problem.*

"Not speaking to me, are you?" she said, lifting her mouth into a smirk.

"I don't want to waste my energy," I replied, trying to push past her.

"You're not even a real Māori," Felicity said.

"What's that supposed to mean?" I asked, I couldn't help myself, anger was burning a giant hole in my chest. "I'm the one who gets to say who I am, and it's none of your flipping business!"

Felicity turned away as if she had lost interest.

I found a desk and sat down, trying to ignore Felicity, but the room started to look grey again, as my mind became full of those thoughts. *I'm all alone, why would anyone want to hang out with me anyway? I must be awful.*

Ella came in and sat down at the desk next to me. She smiled, and I tried to smile back, but I don't think I did it very well.

"How was your weekend?" Ella asked.

Felicity took a step closer to us. "Weekends must suck if you don't have any friends."

I tried to hold in all the feelings – but I couldn't. I stood up and ran out of the classroom before they could see me cry.

I ran straight into the girls' bathrooms and locked myself in a stall, trying to cry silently in case anyone else came in.

"Awa?"

It was Ella's voice.

I didn't say anything.

"Awa, if you're in here…" Ella said. "I'm sorry, Felicity was so mean."

I tried to hold it in, but a big sob came out.

"Awa, come out here," Ella said, her voice was gentle.

"I'll come out soon," I said. "I just need a minute."

"I'll wait," Ella said.

"No – you don't have to do that," I said. "I don't want to make you late." I really wanted to be alone, but she was being so nice.

"It's okay," Ella said. "I take it you didn't have a great weekend?"

"It was… I just had a fight with my best friend Melody – from my old school," I said.

"Oh, that sucks," said Ella.

"Yeah, so when Felicity said that stuff it just…" I didn't know what to say.

"Yeah, I get it," Ella said. "Felicity has been doing that to me for years. That's probably why I don't have any friends, apart from my neighbour."

"You don't?" I asked.

"Not really," Ella said, 'Felicity targets people and gets them to be her friends, or tells them lies about me, so they don't want to be around me."

Now it sounded like Ella was about to cry, her voice had become very high and a bit rough.

I opened the bathroom stall and came out.

"That's awful," I said, looking at my red face in the mirror.

I ran the tap and splashed cold water over my eyes to try to hide that I had been crying.

"I think Felicity is a bit scared of you," Ella said.

"What? Of me?" I asked. "Why?"

"You don't respond like other kids do; you ignore her somehow."

"I react on the inside," I said. "It's like she stirs up all this bad stuff in me, all these horrible thoughts. Apparently, that's anxiety. It makes me quiet; it makes everything look grey."

"That sounds horrible," Ella said, "but anyway, it must scare Felicity, the way you don't respond to her because she *really* doesn't like you."

I sighed, "I've noticed."

"Hey," Ella said, putting her hand on my shoulder. "That's even more reason for us to be friends."

I laughed, "because Felicity hates us both?"

"Because we'll be stronger as friends, and we can support each other."

"That's true, but I don't think that's a good reason," I said.

"Oh," Ella's expression fell into a frown.

"I think there are way better reasons!" I said. "Like –
that you're a nice person, and that we get on well, and
I'm sure we will have lots in common when we get to
know each other better."

Ella smiled.

"I'd like that," she said.

And just like that, I had a friend again.

I gently glided through the tropical rainforest.
Listening to the sound of birdcalls and water droplets
falling from the trees. The sweet scent of tropical
flowers hung in the warm damp air. The plants around
me were brilliant in shades of green with bright pink
flowers. I reached out towards a giant leaf, glistening in
purple dew drops. Something was glowing underneath
it.

I moved the leaf to find.

"You!" I said, startled to see the creature from the
other night. Veila, the dreamcharmer.

"Oh!" Veila was surprised too, just as she had been
in my bedroom. In fact – that was the moment that it
dawned on me that I wasn't in my room back in the
apartment, or even in my world – which had never had
purple dew as far as I could tell.

"Are we… in a dream?" I asked.

"Of course we are," Veila sounded amused as if this
was quite the normal thing.

"But – I'm awake."

"Lucid."

"lu-*what*?!"

"Lucid. It's what we call it when one of you humans seems – well, awake – aware, you know, instead of just wandering in a daze of some sort or another."

"So, this happens a lot?"

"No – not usually – but maybe you are starting to realise you are not usual either."

"I'm floating!" I realised. "Oh my gosh! Where the *hell* are my legs?!" I looked down in panic.

Veila smiled. "You just haven't imagined any legs. You can if you want some…"

I calmed down a bit because it seemed silly to be so freaked out when Veila was so relaxed.

*Imagine legs…* I thought, and looked down to see big hairy legs that looked like they belonged to my dad! "What the…?!"

Veila laughed. "Imagine your own legs," she said.

I tried to imagine what my legs looked like and they appeared below me, looking almost like my normal legs.

"Weird."

"If you say so," Veila said.

"Last time when I met you, you said I was sensitive. What does that mean?" I asked Veila.

"Sensitives have this tendency to feel other people's feelings and absorb their emotions – like a sponge."

"I'm pretty sure I'm human, not sponge," I joked.

"But don't you find you pick up on other people's feelings and after a while, you feel heavy, like you're carrying them around with you? Don't you find you need breaks from people to recover?"

*It's true,* I realised, *I often feel tired after being around people with strong emotions.*

"I thought it was normal," I said.

"There are different levels, and different kinds of sensitivity – most humans can figure out what other people are likely to be feeling based on their tone of voice and stuff, but they don't 'feel' it as if it was their own emotion. Are you also sensitive to light, sound, tastes, smells, that kind of thing?"

"I suppose I am – Mum says I am, except for hot sauce. I put that stuff on everything."

Veila gave me a pointed look and then flipped in the air.

"And... and don't you want to help people – don't you want to stick up for them if things are unfair?'

"Of course I do."

"Even if it's not good for you, personally? Even if you'll get in trouble?"

"Yes..." I wondered what in the world was going on and how I'd ever explain this to my parents.

"And do you feel... kind of different... like you don't really fit in, or belong? Like you were born into the wrong planet or time or country?"

"All the time," I sighed. I didn't even know I could sigh in dreams.

"It sounds to me like you're a sensitive"

"But aren't these things normal?"

"Some of them are normal some of the time, but all of them aren't normal all of the time,"

"Lots of people are sensitive" I said

"Yes – lots of people are sensitive in some ways – but not in every way, and also, most people shut themselves off from anything otherworldly. Most people are scared of the unknown, but you…" Veila said, squinting at me. "You're more scared of the known, aren't you?"

"I'm scared of lots of things… and I guess I am a bit strange, myself."

"You're not scared of me, though, are you?" Veila said, coming closer.

"You're not scary," I said.

"Exactly my point!"

"I still don't understand what you mean by 'a sensitive.'

"You're going to find out – we both are."

"So you don't really know, either?"

"I don't know much, I just know that it's part of my job to find the ones like you, but you are really so rare that you are the first one I've met." Veila peered at me. "Unbelievable!"

CHAPTER SIX

The next day I couldn't stop thinking about the dream creature and how real my dream seemed to be; that was until Mr Jasper rudely interrupted my thoughts with his terrible idea.

"Later this morning," Mr Jasper said, "instead of running around the block, we will be playing basketball."

The kids around me made various kinds of noises. Most of them sounded positive. I felt queasy. I hate sports – especially the kind where there is a ball, and every time it gets thrown in my direction, everyone looks!

I spent the next hour dreading the game, while Mr Jasper got us to read a poem about Narcissus, who was apparently some ancient Greek guy that was so into himself he got trapped looking at his own beautiful reflection. It made me think of Felicity, and the way she often stood in front of the mirrors in the bathroom, putting on lipstick even though we aren't allowed makeup at school.

As we went to get changed into our PE gear, I contemplated all the excuses I could come up with for why I had to leave exactly NOW. *I have a headache, my Mum called, I forgot, my Dad was picking me up to take me to an appointment... I have a medical emergency...* I didn't think Mr Jasper would believe any of this, and so I got into my shorts and T-shirt, my heartbeat hammering in my chest. *I wish we were just running...at least that way no one is looking at me, and I can't mess it up.*

"Are you okay?" Ella asked as we walked out of the changing rooms into the gym.

"Not really," I said. "I hate sports."

Ella's mouth lifted into a small smile. "Me too," she said. At least I wasn't alone.

I put all my effort into carefully avoiding the ball, as much as possible, but I must have gotten distracted because about halfway into the game, a boy with dark hair called out: "Hey."

I looked up, and he threw the ball at me.

I panicked and ducked. The other kids laughed.

"That's not how you play the game, Awa," Felicity said.

My stomach tightened into a knot. Everything around me went grey. I tried to leave the gym, but Mr Jasper stopped me.

"I can't," I said to him, trying to hold back the tears.

"Just hang in there," he said, pushing me back onto the court.

I stood at the edge of the court, frozen, not looking at the game. I didn't care what Felicity and the others thought. I just couldn't...

Finally, Mr Jasper blew his whistle, and it was over.

"Half time!" he said.

*Damn,* I realised, *it's only halfway through!*

The boy with the dark hair came over to where I was standing.

"Hey," he said.

I tried not to look at him.

"I'm sorry," he continued.

"For what?' I asked, looking at my sneakers.

"I didn't realise... when I passed the ball to you. You looked terrified. I didn't mean to do that."

I nodded.

"Look, I'm Evan," he said, holding out his hand. I didn't move. "I'm sorry," he said again. "I'm going to talk to Mr Jasper for you," and he ran off.

*No!*

But it was too late to stop him. He was already talking to the teacher. I heard Mr Jasper disagreeing with him, and Evan using words like "health" and "wellbeing" and "duty of care."

I felt even worse; that was until Mr Jasper waved me over and asked me if I was okay.

"I'm not feeling okay," I admitted.

"You can sit here, on the bench," Mr Jasper said, "but next time, I expect you to try a bit harder, Awa."

I sighed and sat down, just grateful that I didn't have to play that stupid game anymore, at least today.

I was the first back in the changing room, and I was almost dressed by the time Ella came in.

"Are you okay?" Ella asked me again. I just looked at her.

"That was awful," she continued. "Charlie Henson bumped into my chest, and it really hurt. I'm sure he did it on purpose. I wish we could go back to running."

"Me too," I said.

"Hey, that was nice of Evan Chang to talk to Mr Jasper for you."

"Oh, yeah," I said. "That was awkward, but nice."

"He's my neighbour," Ella went on. "Remember how I told you?"

"No."

"Yeah, I told you my only other friend at school was my neighbour – well, that's Evan."

"You don't seem to hang out with him," I said.

"That's because Felicity teases us too much, and so we decided not to hang out at school anymore."

"That's sad," I said, picking up my bag.

"Yeah, you're right," Ella said, "but hey, maybe now you're here, it won't be so bad – you know, power in numbers and all that."

The bell rang for lunch, and we walked out to the tables in the courtyard.

Ella waved Evan over; of course he wanted to know if I was alright, and I was so sick of the question, so instead of answering it, I just said, "Do you want to sit with us?"

"Sure," Evan said, he pulled out his lunch box and

picked up his sandwich. "Want to swap my peanut butter for your ham?" Evan asked Ella.

"In your dreams," she said.

It was nice hanging out with Evan and Ella; they were both so funny and goofy when they were together, I guess they knew each other so well from being friends for practically their whole lives. It made me miss Melody, and the way things used to be, which made me think of my old house and my old life…

"So how are you finding Magnolia Heights?" Evan asked.

"It's… uhh," I tried to find the right words.

"Yeah, tell me about it," Evan smiled.

"It's not that bad," Ella said. "At least there aren't any uniforms."

"It's okay, I guess," I said. "Apart from Felicity."

"She's awful," Ella agreed.

"She's kind of…"

"… racist," Evan said. I nodded.

"You said that before," Ella said. "I never really noticed…"

"Maybe because you're so freaking white," said Evan, gently punching Ella in the shoulder.

"Maybe," Ella said, "or maybe she just never says anything racist in front of other people – that's kind of how her bullying works – she tries to get you when you're alone, to say things that no one else hears, to figure out what things make you feel terrible and then she really twists the knife."

"That sounds about right," I said. "But where does she even get that from?"

"She has a bunch of older siblings," Ella said, it could be one of them.

"Nah – I reckon it's her dad," said Evan. "I've seen the way he glares at me whenever he's picking her up from school."

"Really? People glare at you just because you're not white?" Ella asked. "Oh man, that must be awful."

Evan and I looked at each other.

"You don't say," he said.

"Why didn't you tell me that before?" Ella asked him.

"I don't know – lots of people are racist, it sucks… and that's about it," Evan replied.

"Why don't you tell the teachers," Ella asked, looking at both of us, "or your parents."

"Hah!" I laughed. "There's no way I'd tell Mum anything like that – she'd make such a big deal about it."

"It sucks that you have to deal with it… so much that you never really talked about it," said Ella, looking from me to Evan.

"I don't want it to get me down," Evan said, shrugging, and he smiled at me.

I walked slowly out to the front of the school to wait for Mum to pick me up. That was when I saw him again – the man with the snake tattoo.

I froze.

He was standing right by the school gate, looking in the opposite direction. A chill ran down my spine. *Does he know I'm here? Is it too late to run? He must be looking for me – the snake was just like the one in my nightmare... it's not the first time I've seen him... he must be following me.*

I started backing away, wondering if I would be able to run fast enough. I backed right into someone.

I turned to see Evan, smiling at me.

"Watch where you're going!" he called out, then he saw the serious look on my face.

"What's wrong?" Evan asked.

*How can I explain when the snake man is standing right there?* I wondered. I wished Evan would stay quiet so that the man might not notice me in the sea of other kids leaving school.

"Nothing," I said quietly. "See ya,"

Evan moved past me. *Should I have warned him? I wondered, or is the snake man just after me?*

I looked across to see Evan was talking to him!

I couldn't help it – I just stood there with my mouth open, staring.

"Hey Awa!" Evan called.

*I wish I had the power of invisibility.*

"Come over here!" Evan continued to yell. "Come meet my uncle Pete."

I looked up at the face of the man who had looked so tough and terrifying, only to see a friendly smile.

It turned out that the snake man wasn't waiting for me at all – I was just being paranoid. He was waiting for Evan and was, in fact, Evan's uncle, and actually seemed quite nice. I talked to them for a while before Mum arrived. On the drive home I wondered how I had been so wrong about that guy – why did I jump to conclusions and think he was evil? How did I misread the signs so badly?

The next few days went past in a blur. I hadn't had the chance to talk to Ella much. She never seemed to be around at breaks. It was almost as if she was avoiding me.

Evan had started to talk to me more, so at least I wasn't completely alone, but I didn't feel like I had any real friends at this school.

I missed Melody, which also made me miss my old house, and even my old school. I had one less problem though: Felicity hadn't spoken to me lately, which was great.

The bell rang for the end of the day on Friday, and I saw Ella packing up. Everyone else had already left the classroom. They must have packed up before the bell even rang.

"Hey," I said. "Are you feeling okay?"

"I'm not sick if that's what you mean," Ella said. She smiled, but it didn't seem to be a real smile.

"I was starting to think you were avoiding me. I've hardly seen you all week." I said.

"It's just…" Ella looked down at the floor, and I realised there *was* something wrong. *What did I do?* I wondered; *did I offend her somehow?*

"It's not you," Ella said. "I've just been feeling really weird and…" she looked around again. "Do you want to go and get a shake?"

"Sure," I said. I was curious to know what was going on, and it wasn't like I had any other plans.

We walked out of the school together, and Ella seemed to relax. It wasn't until we had ordered our chocolate shakes at the ice cream parlour down the road that she started talking.

"Okay, the thing is, I have this crush, and it's driving me nuts."

Ella looked at me, testing to see if I was going to laugh at her.

"I hate it when that happens!" I said, throwing my arms up in an exaggerated way. This was kind of a lie because I didn't really get crushes, but I knew they were a pain. Melody was always crushing on different people in our old class and being dramatic about it.

"Do you?" Ella looked at me. "I mean, do you like anyone at school?"

I blushed. It wasn't because I did like anyone, but because I was a bit ashamed to admit that I never got crushes, as if there was something wrong with me.

"I only just got here!" I said.

"Yes, but you blushed," Ella said.

"It's just an awkward question," I told her. "I honestly swear that I don't have any crushes."

*At all.*

"Okay," Ella said. "It's just that... I think Evan likes you."

I could see from the pain in Ella's eyes that this was a problem, not just for me (because AWKWARD) but for her, because obviously Evan was the one she had a crush on.

"The feeling's not mutual," I assured her. "He's okay, as a friend, but..."

"He's not your type?" Ella said, the spark returning to her eyes.

"I guess not." We both took big sips of our shakes. They were delicious.

"So..." Ella said, really smiling now. "What is bothering you then?"

"Is it that easy to tell?" I asked. "I guess everything is. I miss my old house and even my old school!"

"And your friends?"

"I guess... and Mum is really stressed. I hardly see Dad. Also, I've been having these weird dreams."

I figured it was okay to tell her a little bit, without sounding totally crazy.

"I don't even remember my dreams," Ella said.

"I didn't use to, either," I said.

It was true. Before recently, everything was a blur when I woke up – with just pieces left behind, like the bits of plastic and sand-polished glass you find on a beach, parts of a puzzle from a story you will never know. "Now, I remember every last detail."

"Are they scary?" Ella asked. "Like nightmares?"

"Not always... just really strange," I said.

"That's pretty cool, like free entertainment. You should write them down."

I laughed. "I wouldn't even know where to start!" It felt good being able to talk to someone about this, even if I couldn't tell her the whole truth.

"Have you ever..." I started. "Have you ever had a dream where you were kind of awake in it?"

"You mean like a lucid dream?" Ella asked.

*Lucid,* my mind started to spin. I almost knocked over my shake.

"Is that a real word?" I asked. I had only heard it in my dream, from that strange glowing creature.

"Sure," Ella said. "My brother used to have them sometimes. He even trained himself to have them. He said he liked to fly in his dreams – but it was more like taking really big jumps, slowly... into the air."

*No way...Not only did those dreams feel real, they were also using real words that I don't even know!*

"Are you okay?" Ella asked me. "You look pale. Too much shake?"

"Sorry – I just remembered I was supposed to meet my Mum," I lied. "I hope you have a good weekend!"

I got up and left the ice cream parlour. I couldn't trust myself not to be weird around Ella when there was so much going on in my head.

*How is this possible?* I wondered as I walked home. *Lucid... It's obviously not a common word.* Maybe I had heard the word before and had just somehow forgotten that I knew it. *I could have seen it in a movie or something.* I tried to reassure myself, but I went around in circles. There were only two possibilities: *Either I'm going crazy, or my dreams are... real.*

CHAPTER SEVEN

*I* was so tired when I went to sleep that night. Mum said it had been a long week, and she was right. It didn't help that she kept bringing up that she wanted me to see a shrink.

"It might help, honey," she insisted.

I wasn't convinced. I just felt awful, but at least she didn't tell me to turn the lights out these days. I had won that argument – for now – but tonight I felt brave, so I just had my little night light on. Maybe I would get a better sleep and have better dreams!

I drifted off to sleep, wondering if I would ever meet Veila again... and I was also worried about how much the shrink would cost when Mum was already broke, and how awkward it would be to talk to a stranger, and how they obviously would also think I was crazy if I told them the truth.

The carnival spread out all around me – rust-coloured and shifting like a magic-eye. The scent of grease hung in the air. I had a feeling I had been there before.

Crowds bustled past me with candy floss and popcorn. People were throwing strange things at large red and white targets: handbags, road cones, live rats.

Eugh… yuck!

I backed away.

I had the creeping feeling that I was being watched again. I started running, faster and faster, through the crowds, out of the carnival, to the edge of the cliff. The sea spread out in front of me in both directions. I looked down at my feet. The ground was crumbling.

*No!*

I was falling.

The terror rose up as I fell.

I woke in my bed, a garbled noise coming from my mouth as I tried to scream in my sleep. As my heartbeat slowed back to normal, I reassured myself:

*Just a falling dream... Nothing unusual about that.* I'd had them before, lots of times. It was actually kind of a relief, like, *hey, I can still dream normally!*

I rolled over and drifted back to sleep; I was in the carnival again, but it was empty, and this time I was awake in my dream; I was lucid.

I remembered what Ella had said about her brother flying in his dreams, so I thought I would give it a try. I lifted my arms and took a big jump. I kept rising, slowly, higher, and higher. I felt that roller-coaster feeling in my gut, the one when you're going up so high that you get butterflies about coming down.

I wasn't flying like superman; it was more like a big, slow bounce that took me up, up, up, over the carnival, and then slowly back down.

*I guess gravity works differently here.* I jumped from building to building, from hill to hill. It was fun looking at the shifting changing view of the carnival city all around me.

*What is this place?* I wondered. It looked familiar but strange, as though my mind had just made it up randomly by piecing together other things I'd seen before.

I drifted back down to the middle of the carnival to have a look. It was still deserted, which made it seem spooky.

"Hello!" I called out.

I heard a bang and a creaking noise.

"Is someone there?"

I had the creepy feeling I was being watched. *Not again!* I started walking – not running. *Running shows you're scared.* I walked fast as if I was busy and had things to do.

I saw a glimmer in the corner of my eye and turned to find…

"Veila?"

She was hovering in front of a stall of clown faces with open mouths – you know the kind you're supposed to throw things into to win prizes, only I knew there were no prizes in this strange place, at least none I would want to win!

"There you are!" she said. "I've been looking all over for you."

"Was it you," I looked around, "following me?"

"I just got here," Veila said. She looked back in the direction I had come from.

"Shall we leave this place?" she asked.

"Where do you want to go?"

"Deeper into the Dreamrealm; there's not much work to do here."

"What is this place?" I asked. "And what kind of work are you talking about?"

"Dreamwork, silly!" she said, smiling at me. "And this place is what you humans would think of as an ordinary dreaming place if you thought very much about it at all. It's what we call the Rooms of Mind."

"We're not in any rooms," I pointed out. "We're outside."

"Are you so sure about that?" Veila asked, grabbing my hand with her tiny glowing fingers sending nice shivers up my arm.

She led me to the door. It was an ordinary-looking door, painted blue; only it didn't seem to be attached to anything. It was just standing in the middle of the path.

"Open it," she said.

I laughed. "It's just a propped-up door; we can walk around it."

"Oh no, that won't get you anywhere useful," Veila insisted. "Open it."

"Okay," I said, and laughed, mostly because I thought it was a funny thing to do. I turned the knob and pushed the door wide open, expecting to see the same thing through it as all around it – the skyline around the carnival, only...

"What?!"

Behind the door was a dark hallway.

"No way!"

"Let's go!" she said and pulled me inside. I closed the door and took a closer look at the hallway.

"I guess this is just a dream," I said.

Veila laughed as if that was the most hysterical thing she had ever heard.

"Just a dream. Oh my!" she said. "You don't believe in dreams."

"Of course I do," I said.

"Oh no, you think they aren't real."

"Well..."

"Never mind, you'll see soon enough."

We started moving down the hallway for what felt like a very long time, turning corners into other similar hallways.

"Does this go on forever?"

"Forever is a funny thing to say," Veila said.

"Do... other people come here when they are dreaming?" I wondered.

"Not much," Veila replied. "Most humans dream in the Rooms of Mind – in whichever room they find themselves in, not many find the hallway."

"So, where are we going?" I asked.

"You'll see," Veila said, she slowed down as she approached a door. I realised there were doors all along the hallway; I just hadn't seen them before. Maybe I wasn't paying attention, or maybe they hadn't been there a second ago.

"Shall we go into one of those rooms?" I asked.

"They're not all rooms," Veila replied. "But sure – pick one"

I heard a muffled noise from behind a door to my left, which was slightly ajar. I pushed it open to find a large pile of multi-coloured mattresses reaching up into the white ceiling. At the top of the pile, ten metres high was a golden throne, and on that throne sat a very odd figure, small and squat with shoulder-length brown hair.

"Hello?" I said. "Who are you?"

"I am special."

The voice was deeper than I expected.

"Special?" I asked.

"I am special. I must be chosen…"

The voice sped up as if it was on fast-forward, becoming much higher in pitch.

"…because I am special."

"Is that your name?" I asked, curious about this strange being on a mattress throne.

"All the names belong to ME!"

"She's a splinter," Veila whispered. "A part that has splintered off from the Whole."

"Like a splinter in my foot?" I wondered out loud.

"Exactly – so she gets stuck, and she's irritating," said Veila.

"Don't call me that," the splinter growled.

"They prefer to be called 'fragments'," said Veila.

"I prefer special!" the fragment said.

We backed out of the room and continued down the hallway, past doors in various colours. My mind was swimming with questions that I couldn't quite put into words.

"Open this one," Veila instructed.

"Okay," I said, wondering if she couldn't open them herself.

The door opened to reveal a sunset view. We were up high, looking down on the ocean. The hills around us were bathed in orange light.

"If you want to come with me – you just have to trust," Veila said.

"Trust what?" I asked, realizing that I hardly knew anything about this small glowing creature, and here she was telling me to trust her.

*Do I? I've followed her this far, haven't I?*

"Trust enough that when we fall, we carry on."

We had reached the edge of the cliff.

"We need to fall off the cliff?" I gulped. This seemed pretty extreme.

"It's more about trusting than it is about falling."

"What does the trust do?"

"It carries us through to the other side of the Dreamrealm – where things are not so random and confusing, where we are deeper into being."

That did sound better than the way things had been so far, but could I really trust her? What if she was dangerous? What if she was evil? I looked at her little shining face. It made no sense in my head, but my gut reaction was to trust her.

"Okay," I said.

"But we can't go now."

"Why not?" I felt a bit disappointed – strangely.

"Because you are too afraid to fall. It only works here if you are not afraid," she said.

"I can't help that, though," I said.

It seemed like there was a real purpose to all of this, and if I could only get to the other side, I could get away from the confusion and figure out what was going on... *only now, she won't let me.*

"No, but we can play," Veila said, she opened her mouth wide and began to sing a little song:

*When the fruit is ripe, it will fall,*
*Not through any effort at all*
*By being ready to let go.*
*At the right time, it knows!*

"Whatever that means," I muttered to myself.

"Here," Veila reached out and grabbed at the air. A rope-swing appeared that had definitely not been there just before.

"Let's play!"

We swung on the rope, around and around until I was dizzy, higher and higher; the butterflies fluttered in my stomach again. I tipped my head back and relaxed, enjoying the upside-down sunset as it swam in and out of focus in front of me.

Veila looked at me. "You're ready now," she said.

I thought of her song. *I don't need to try... I just need to let go.*

I let go…

…and fell.

Instead of terrifying, it was fantastically exhilarating!

I woke – but instead of waking to my bedroom, I found myself lying on the dark, cold floor in the pitch black. The air was thick and still.

"Veila?" I called out. There was no response. "Veila?! Where are you?"

I lay there, terrified, not knowing where I was or what was around me in that heavy darkness.

*Calm down; it's okay.* I told myself. *It will all be okay.*

Up above, I saw a tiny light, like a firefly. It got bigger as it moved closer until I recognised…

"Veila!" I said. "Thank goodness!"

"It takes me a while to get down," she explained. "I don't fall, I float."

"Where are we?"

"Almost there," she said.

I stood up and followed her. I could tell from her glow that we were nearing the faint outline of another door.

"Open it," she said.

I pushed at the door and was blinded by the light

behind it.

"What is this place?" I asked, as my eyes adjusted. I was looking out through the doorframe into a world, unlike any other I had ever seen.

All around us were bright green hills, speckled with dazzling colours, and up above the sky was... *Purple!*

"This is the meadow," Veila replied. "Welcome to the Dreamrealm.

"Wow!"

The air was so still, compared to the strong Wellington winds, but it wasn't just the lack of wind – there was a deep sense of calm like I've never known before – a kind of tranquil peacefulness.

There was only the slight hint of a breeze on my skin, making shimmery ripples in the vivid green grass that stretched out over the gently rolling hills towards the spiralling purple sky.

As I stepped through the door, I had the strange sensation that I was expanding, like a balloon being filled with helium. I didn't realise how heavy my life had been feeling until that moment when it was suddenly light – like I could float all around this peaceful shimmering place and never need to worry about a thing ever again.

"Is this... is this like a level of the heavens?" I asked Veila. My great-aunt Rosetta used to tell me stories about the atua, the Māori gods, and how some of them lived in the twelve heavens.

"Could be," said Veila. "What's a heaven?"

"It's..." my voice trailed off as I got distracted again

by the shimmering colours all around us – so intense and brilliant – and so real! – more real than anything I'd ever seen in my life. I looked out across the meadow to see hundreds of pink jellyfish gliding gracefully through the sky; a patch of what looked like multi-coloured flowers took flight, becoming a spectacular cloud of butterflies; bubbles the size of basketballs drifted lazily around, before bursting into stunning sparkles in the air.

The more I looked, the more details I noticed, or maybe they just changed right in front of my eyes. Even the surface of the luxurious green grass shifted into different patterns as if it was somehow reflecting a delightful kaleidoscope.

"No way," I said, trying to take in all the astonishing things. "This is impossible!"

"What a silly thing to say," Veila said, hovering next to me. "There is no impossible… only different shades of possible."

"But it isn't real," I insisted. "It's just a dream."

"Of course it is a dream," said Veila, "and *of course* it is real. What is it with you humans – assuming that only the things you see when you're awake are real?"

Everything seemed to shift – just as I looked at it, and I had this feeling like anything was possible – even more than that – probable – as if everything I wanted was somehow within reach.

"It's so different out here," I said, looking back to see whatever it was I had just walked out of. The building was made of a series of interconnected domes.

"The Rooms of Mind?" I wondered out loud.

"Yes," Veila responded. "Until now, you were exploring the Rooms of Mind – which is where most people dream."

"Why am I here, then?" I asked as I continued to stare at the breath-taking view of the meadow all around me. "If most people just dream in there, why am I outside?"

"You're a sensitive, which makes it easier for you to navigate the Dreamrealm. There is much more than you humans usually see – you were going around the usual dream spaces in there," she gestured to the dome buildings. "They seem to transform to reflect what people project from their heads."

"Seem to?"

"Yes," Veila said. "They are blank, otherwise. If I go in there by myself, they are mostly just a series of white rooms, with the occasional fragment that has wandered in there to make a nest."

"But surely we can't all be in there – every single dreaming human, all at the same time?"

"Why not?"

"It's too small!" I said. "We would be squished up against each other with even a small fraction of the population."

"First of all, you assume dreaming is not real, and now you assume it follows the same rules as waking!" Veila said, laughing at me.

I looked around at the horizon at all the colours and patterns, swirling and glowing.

"Wait, is this place even on earth?" I asked.

"Not in the way you might think," Veila said, looking at me, curiously.

"Then, in what way?"

"It's undecided," Veila said. "It can't be in any one place at once – it can only be in many places simultaneously… so the answer is always yes and no."

"That makes no sense," I said.

"There you go with your boring assumptions again!" said Veila, flipping around in the air.

I looked down to see I had no feet or legs again. I closed my eyes and imagined them into being, then I walked, barefoot on the soft grass. It felt amazing under my toes; a warm feeling spread all the way through me.

I sighed.

"It's so beautiful here!" I said, enjoying the light breeze on my skin, bringing with it the scent of fresh spring blossoms. "And it's so much more peaceful than back there," I gestured to the domed building.

"I feel like running!" I said, and began to sprint down a hill. I ran until I collapsed on the soft, squishy grass, looking up at the swirl of purple sky, brightened by the golden sun.

I was wonderfully calm and happy, so unlike how I usually felt at home or school. My mind was clear – my thoughts were sharp and bright instead of muddled and fuzzy – *whatever this feeling is, it's the exact opposite of anxiety!*

"I wish I could stay here," I said to Veila.

"You can come back," Veila said, coming to rest beside me, on the grass. "We might need you to."

"What do you mean?"

"I told you, sensitives are very rare. They have certain abilities that most humans don't have. They can help with the dreamweaving."

"I don't understand what that is."

"All in good time," said Veila again.

"I just wish I had proof that this was real!" I said.

I saw a sparkle of light in the corner of my eye and looked out to see a glimmer of gold on the other side of the meadow.

Just then, my foot struck against something hard; I looked down to see a boulder that I was sure wasn't there a moment before; pain shot through my ankle, and I lost my balance.

*I'm falling!*

Just as I was about to hit the ground, I woke with a jolt in my bed, my heart pounding.

I reached for my ankle.

"Ouch!" I touched the place where, only moments before, it had hit the boulder.

*I hurt myself in the Dreamrealm, and it carried through to my waking life.*

There was no way I could have gotten a sore ankle from anything in my soft bed. I had asked for proof, and I had received it.

*The Dreamrealm is real!*

## CHAPTER EIGHT

The feeling of magic stayed with me the next morning, even though my foot was still sore from when I had fallen in the dream, and I was walking with a little limp. I was also relieved that I had an excuse to avoid basketball games for a while. I told Mum that I must have fallen over and hurt it during school sports, and she wrote me a note.

As I walked out of the school gates after class, I was too busy thinking about the Dreamrealm and how it *has to be real.* I didn't even realise that someone was waiting for me.

"Awa," said a man's voice. I almost jumped out of my skin.

"Dad!" It wasn't that I didn't know my own dad's voice; it was just that I wasn't expecting him. "What are you doing here?" I asked.

"It's good to see you too, honey," Dad said, shaking his head. His dark, straight hair shined in the sunlight. I had always wished I looked more like Dad with his naturally straight hair – his Chinese heritage didn't quite carry that gene through to me.

"You need a haircut," I said, reaching up to ruffle his hair.

"*You* can talk," Dad said, smiling and messing my hair up too.

"It is good to see you!" I said, giving him a big hug. "I just… I didn't know you would be here. It's been…"

"Yeah, I know," Dad said, looking down. "It's been too long, and I'm sorry. You know, work has been crazy, and the move was hard."

"Dad, you moved months ago," I said. I didn't want to let him off the hook – not with such a lame excuse.

He looked at me. "I'm sorry, Awa," he said. "There has been a lot going on, but I'm here now. How about we go out for pizza like I promised?"

"I can't say no to pizza," I said.

It didn't take long for me to forgive Dad for not making more of an effort to spend time with me. It was so good to see him. He told me about work being crazy busy, and about some new gadgets he had ordered online and how he hadn't even unpacked at his new place yet because things had been so hectic. I could imagine Dad's apartment full of boxes; Mum always said he was a bit of a hoarder, like me.

We walked the couple of blocks to Toni's Pizza, our favourite place. Once we had ordered a large pepperoni pizza with extra chili, we sat down at a booth and opened our sodas.

"Listen, Awa," Dad said. "There's something I need to talk to you about."

A whole load of freaky thoughts crashed through my mind: *Dad is moving overseas, he's met someone new, and they are getting married; I don't even know my new step-mother, and she's going to be a nightmare; he's having another child; he's sick, sick with cancer and dying; Mum's sick; we are all sick...*

Obviously, my heart was racing by this point; everything was going grey.

"Don't look so worried," Dad said.

"Are you going to survive?" I asked.

"What?! Nothing's wrong with me," Dad said.

"Is... is Mum okay?"

"Mum's fine,"

"Are you having another kid?"

"What? No!"

I let out a sigh of relief; I wasn't prepared for that.

"It's actually you we are worried about, Awa," Dad said. "Your Mum called me and told me you are having problems with anxiety again, especially at school..."

"Oh," I said blushing. I wish Mum hadn't gone and talked to Dad about that behind my back!

"I'm fine, Dad," I said. "Really."

The pizza arrived on the table, and we just looked at each other, not quite ready to eat because we were too busy having 'real talk' I guess.

I took a gulp of my soda and picked up a big slice of pizza. This conversation sure wasn't helping my anxiety, but at least there was hot melted cheese right in front of me.

As I stuffed the pizza in my mouth, Dad said, "Your mother said you are having scary dreams too. She's worried about you."

"They're just dreams, Dad," I lied.

*Curse Mum for telling him!*

"She said you seem to be having trouble telling your dreams apart from reality," Dad continued.

*That's because they ARE real*, I thought, but I wasn't about to tell him that. I stuffed more pizza into my face. Dad still hadn't eaten any.

"Look, Awa, remember when it got bad last time?" he said. "When you found out about the divorce and everything…"

I nodded, but I didn't say anything because my mouth was too full.

"Remember how we went to the doctor, Doctor Gilles, and he said that if it got worse we could get you some special help… someone to talk to?"

"I remember," I said, finally. "And Mum has already asked me."

"So, let's give it a try," Dad said, gently.

"I'm fine, Dad, really… I was just having a weird day. Mum must have misunderstood me – you know what she's like."

Dad's face became serious. "Yes, I know what she's like."

"You really don't have to worry about me – I don't

need a shrink!" I said and laughed, but Dad's face remained serious.

"Let's just give it a try, Awa," Dad said. "I know things can be... difficult with your mother, believe me!"

"This isn't about her," I said, I didn't want him to think she was making me crazy or anything.

"We'll see... what the doctor says," Dad said. "I just want you to be safe and well, honey. That's all."

I sighed. "Okay," I said. Dad had this way of convincing me that I didn't quite understand. "I'll give it a try."

"Great," Dad said and picked up the biggest slice of pizza. "I've got some catching up to do!" he said – gesturing to the half-empty box.

*Yes, yes you do, Dad.*

After the pizza, we walked down to the Waterfront and sat by the sea. The air smelled like Wellington always does – like salt and coffee and mildew. It was so good, just hanging out with Dad. I tried not to think about having to see the psychiatrist. We sat there for ages, just talking and watching the seagulls swoop and dive around the harbour. It was the happiest I had been in months, other than in my dreams, but my mind kept drifting back to the meadow and hoping that I could go there again.

I went to sleep that night, thinking of Veila – and just kind of willing myself to find her, wherever she was.

# CHAPTER NINE

The carnival hummed with life around me. There was a buzzing sound and the smell of hot dogs in the air. People moved through the stalls, but there was something bizarre going on. I looked closer.

*Their faces!*

There was something wrong with their faces. It was hard to focus; I squinted into the light, looking at the adults and children surrounding me.

*Their faces are blank!*

I started to run, but the ground seemed to dissolve beneath my feet. I wasn't moving anywhere. The faceless people turned towards me.

"I'm special! I'm special!" a voice behind me called out.

I didn't turn towards the voice. I already knew who it belonged to. Another sound broke through: a hissing sound like a snake. I didn't want to see what was making that sound either!

I ran – faster and faster. This time the ground was stable underfoot, but something was blocking the path, something familiar.

A blue door!

That was when I realised where I was – *in a dream* – and I knew exactly how to get out of this place.

I ran towards the door. It swung open, and I crashed straight into…

"Veila?"

"There you are!" Veila said. Her voice sounded grumpy as if she had been looking for me all day.

I followed her down the dark hallway. Veila opened a door that led straight into the meadow, this time.

I sighed in relief at the warm floating feeling which spread right through me again, as I stepped out into the soft spongy grass, breathing in the fresh blossomy scent of the meadow. There were no clouds of jellyfish or butterflies this time, just the unmistakable purple swirling sky above.

There were a few other differences too. An old-fashioned lamppost stood nearby as if it had always been there. I was going to ask about it when I saw something more interesting:

*A woman and a lion?*

They sat together in quite a friendly way. The woman's vivid green eyes sparkled in the sunshine, and her long, flowing orange hair glistened, full of star-shaped flowers. She seemed to be making a daisy chain, maybe for her lion friend.

I couldn't explain it; part of me wanted to rush forward – to befriend them, but something else pulled me back. Perhaps, like most other things in this place, they weren't what they seemed.

"Who are they?" I asked Veila, I couldn't stop staring, although neither the woman or the lion seemed to notice us at all.

"That is Strength," said Veila.

"Strength?" I asked. "Which one?"

"The usual one," Veila replied.

I turned to look at Veila for a moment, trying to work out what she meant, and by the time I glanced back, the woman and the lion had both vanished, and so had the lamppost, as if they'd never been there.

"Were you looking for me?" I asked Veila. "In the carnival?"

"Of course I was," she replied. "We need your help. Sensitives are so rare. They are the only ones who can help us in the dreamwork, the work of the Chalice of Cosmos, the Shadow work."

"What is that?"

"It is alchemy, but not as you know it."

Alchemy made me think of olden days scientists trying to turn lead into gold... *and I'm pretty sure that's not what we were doing here.*

"Veila, what is the Shadow?" I asked.

Veila trembled causing a chill to run down my spine like it was contagious. I got the feeling that she didn't want me to ask any more about that particular topic.

I remembered the chalice from my dream.

"I think I've been there," I said. "To the chalice, I mean."

"How could you possibly have been there?" Veila said, floating so close to my face that she was almost touching my nose. I stepped back. *Haven't dream-charmers ever heard of personal space?!*

I looked down at my hand to see the sparkle was still there, on my fingernail – at least it was now, in my dream, even though it had faded from my real hand.

"It's why my nail looks like this!" I said, holding out my hand.

Veila gasped. "I don't believe it!"

"Anyway," I said, "how can I help you if I keep waking up? How can I do this if it's so… patchy?"

What I really wanted was to be able to get back to the meadow in my dreams all the time.

It was so wonderful and so peaceful there. I lay back and looked up at the sky, I could see giant birds flying overhead. They looked a bit like seagulls but much, *much* larger… or maybe that was just something to do with the swirling sky distorting my perspective.

"If you want to get back here," Veila said, "you need to eat some of the fruit of the Elisiad tree."

"Yes, I do – I will!" I said, practically jumping for joy at the thought that I could come back here every night. "How do I find it?"

"I'll show you," Veila said.

She guided me up a hill. It was steep, and the grass seemed to become longer as we walked, shifting underfoot like I was sinking into warmed butter. The scent of jasmine hung heavy in the air as I climbed, up and up… It felt like hours, until finally Veila pointed up ahead.

Around us stretched vast dark forest, glimmering with thousands of glowing things. A spectacular tree stood at its edge; the tallest tree by far, its branches reached up into the sky. Something about its shape and leaves was familiar.

"How are we supposed to get the fruit?" I asked Veila.

"It's like I said," she replied. "When the fruit is ripe, it drops. We can't force the tree to share its fruit. Just wait."

She started to sing her song again.

*When the fruit is ripe, it will fall,*
*Not through any effort at all*
*By being ready to let go.*
*At the right time, it knows!*

I rested against the tree and closed my eyes. Thoughts swirled in my head. Everything had been so intense and dazzling… and confusing. Eventually, as I rested there, my mind started to feel calm and relaxed.

I heard a small thud in front of me and opened my eyes to find a bunch of purple berries.

"The fruit of Elisiad!" Veila said

"They're… so beautiful," I looked at the wondrous purple berries that seemed to glow, with their own inner light. They swirled with a depth that looked like stars.

"They remind me a bit of the chalice."

"The Chalice of Cosmos?" Veila said. "Yes – they are connected, as all things are connected. These are fruits of wisdom and connection."

*Not more cryptic messages!*

"What happens to me if I eat them?" I asked.

"You'll be able to come here more easily – you will be guided by your own sense of being in a much stronger way."

"That sounds good," I said. "What do they taste like?"

"I have no idea," Veila said. "We don't eat them."

"Then how do you know they are safe?"

"Sometimes, you just have to trust and let go…" Veila said.

I reached out tentatively and plucked a berry, the size of a sparrow's egg.

It smelled good, reminding me of a warm summer's day.

I bit into it, releasing sweet, tangy juice into my mouth like nothing I had ever tasted before. It was exquisite; it sent shivers down my spine and brought me visions of open horizons at dawn, of waterfalls, of crystals, of flames flickering on an open fire. I sighed. The juice of the fruit seemed to be absorbing right through my mouth into my blood and bone, working its magic into my brain, into my genetic code. I ate another berry and another. I could not stop until I had eaten the entire bunch, and only then did I feel completely satisfied.

I sat for what felt like a long time, resting under the tree in the cool breeze.

Eventually, I turned to Veila. "So now that I've eaten the berries, I will find it easier to get here – to do this dreamwork?"

"Almost," Veila said. "When you are ready, a way will be made."

"What does that mean?" It sounded like an old saying.

"Look around you," Veila said. "Notice anything different?"

I looked around properly. "Actually, everything looks a bit different. The sky looks even more shimmery. The grass is a deeper green than before. Is that possible?"

"Anything is possible," Veila responded. "Do you see anything that wasn't there before?"

I scanned the view and noticed something in the grass: a lighter part of it that seemed to lead down the hill towards the forest. "Wait, is that a path?" I asked.

"Have a closer look."

I got up, and Veila followed me over to what was more clearly visible now as a cobbled path.

"I'm sure it was made of grass just a minute ago," I said. What had stopped looking like glass, on closer inspection, was thousands of smooth green stones – a similar shape to the ones Dad liked to skip over the water.

"Sometimes things are there and yet not visible," Veila explained. "The deeper we grow the more we see."

Shivers ran down my spine. I reached the path and began to follow it. It felt as if I was being guided along. It felt like gliding, almost like a slow, gentle slide, down, down, into the forest, then deeper, deeper...

On closer inspection, the glowing things I'd noticed in the forest earlier were actually mushrooms and toadstools growing all over the forest floor, emitting their own light.

"Where are we going?" I asked Veila.

"You'll see."

I had never seen so many unusual plants and trees... some of them seemed to glimmer and shimmer around me.

*Maybe it's just the berries, but this place is amazing.*

The forest became deeper and darker as I moved along; with fewer glowing toadstools, the darkness became ominous and menacing. I was glad for the path that glowed with its own light; I was afraid to move away from it, even with Veila's company, it felt like only by staying on these green stones would I be safe.

Up ahead, I noticed a light and moved towards it, along the path, grateful to get away from the darkness.

"It looks like a clearing, ahead," I said to Veila.

"It does indeed," Veila replied, her voice rising in excitement.

As we reached the edge of the clearing, I heard the sound of a gently flowing stream, along with sweet melodies of birdsong. The scent of honeysuckle wafted in the air. I stepped into the light and with it came a zillion tiny tingles, running like electricity through every cell in my body, and the feelings of the night before Christmas I'd had as a child.

Butterflies in rainbow colours danced around the circle of big trees with purplish leaves. Wildflowers seemed to spring up all around us. I gasped at the exquisiteness of it all. "It's so lovely. Where are we?"

"The Grove," Veila said. "It's a special place."

"It feels special."

At the centre of the Grove were several big flat dusty-green boulders of the same kind of stone as the path. I moved towards them, noticing a pond at their centre, from which a small stream flowed.

"You can sit down," Veila said, "and I will give you the instructions."

"The instructions?"

"On how to get back here."

"Oh?"

"You said you wanted to come more easily into the Dreamrealm – out of the Rooms of Mind, which are so confusing."

"Yes… so I could come here instead, from the waking world?" I wanted it so much I could hardly contain myself; to arrive into the Grove, this magnificent place – to spend more time here, where even just being here for a few moments, I seemed to soak up good feelings that eased my worries and refreshed me.

"Yes," Veila said. "I will teach you how to get back here – although there is a possibility you could get distracted on your way and be diverted someplace else, so pay attention."

"Okay." I sat on one of the big green rocks. Its surface was cool and smooth and relaxing, somehow.

"Close your eyes."

I did.

"Okay, now breathe slowly. Count to four as you breathe in, and then count to six as you breathe out."

I felt myself breathe in. *One, two, three, four.* Then out, *one, two three, four, five, six.* I did this three times, as Veila instructed.

"Now say: I am water, earth, sun, and sky."

"I am water, earth, sun, and sky."

"I am dawn, noon, dusk and midnight."

"I am dawn, noon, dusk and midnight."

"I am the whisper in the wind..."

"I am the whisper in the wind..."

"... and I am here."

"... and I am here."

I opened my eyes to bright sunlight. I looked around my bedroom wondering if the spell had worked both ways – *Did I just summon myself into my waking life?*

# CHAPTER TEN

*I* had my first appointment with Dr Spancer the next day, but my head was so full of thoughts about Veila and the Dreamrealm, and the long weekend and my sleepover with Ella later that day, that I didn't really want to go and talk to some random doctor about my brain.

Dr Spancer had grey hair and glasses, but her face looked younger than her hair. I didn't feel like saying much in that small, bare office. She asked a lot of questions about my parents.

"It's not about them," I said.

It wasn't my parents making me anxious. It was everything else.

"So, tell me, Awa," Dr Spancer said, lowering her glasses. "Why are you here?"

"I don't know. They're just worried," I said.

"What is really bothering you?"

I couldn't tell her that...especially not since all my

worries seemed insignificant after my recent most wonderful dreams, but I had to say something.

"It's just… everything feels hard and confusing… and pointless," I said.

"What do you think is the point?"

"What do you mean?" I asked.

"What do you believe in… do you think we are here for a reason?" Dr Spancer asked.

"I don't know," I said. "We're not really God people." It was something my dad, the atheist, usually said.

Dr Spancer nodded and wrote something down.

"So tell me more about these dreams you've been having, who is in them?"

I looked at Dr Spancer for a moment. I wanted to tell someone about my dreams; they were too exciting to keep all to myself… and even if she didn't believe me, what did I really have to lose?

"These sessions are confidential, right?" I asked.

The doctor nodded.

"Well, there is someone – she's kind of like a fairy."

"A fairy?" Dr Spancer's eyes widened.

"Uhh, not really, she doesn't have wings."

"And what does she do?" Dr Spancer asked.

"Well, I saw her in my room once" I said, and explained how I had met Veila.

"And that was the only time you've seen her?"

"While I was awake," I said, trying not to make it sound too confusing. I didn't really know how to explain any of this to anyone, but it did feel good to talk about it – like the pressure of keeping it to myself was being released.

"You think you were really awake?" the doctor raised her eyebrows and frowned.

"Yes – but I see her in my dreams, too."

"How often?" Dr Spancer glanced up from her notepad giving me that look – the same one my parents both had when I talked to them about anything weird.

"Every night, almost," *...except for when I get stuck in the random dreams, or when she isn't around.*

Dr Spancer raised her eyebrows. The fluorescent ceiling light glinted off her spectacles and silvery hair.

"What do you think she is? A fairy... but not a fairy?"

"She's a dreamcharmer."

Something seemed to stir in Dr Spancer's eyes. "*Déjà vu,*" she muttered to herself.

"What?"

"Nothing," she said, loosening her collar and pulling at the sleeves of her peach coloured cardigan.

"Awa, I'm going to teach you some breathing techniques, to manage the anxiety at school, but these dreams..." her voice trailed off. "I'm concerned that they are scaring you, and that it's sometimes hard to tell the difference between being awake and being asleep."

I just looked at the doctor; it was clear she hadn't really listened to me at all. I kept my mouth shut and vowed to keep it that way.

"I will talk to your parents about prescribing you some pills to help with the dreams."

*No, I will NOT be taking them.*

I kept my mouth shut and looked at the floor.

I waited outside while my parents talked to the doctor. I looked at the old children's books (too young for me) and the old magazines (too old), and scuffed my feet on the carpet and chewed my nails until the door opened a crack and Mum started to walk through.

I heard the doctor's voice drifting out: "Again, there's probably nothing to worry about... many children have imaginary friends at her age."

My heart sank. So that was all – imaginary – well... *I'll never bother talking to adults ever again.*

Before we left the clinic Doctor Spancer gave my parents a prescription for pills that might help the dreams go away.

"I'm *not* going to take them," I insisted as we walked out towards Mum's car.

"Just give them a try," Dad said.

Mum looked at me; her eyes were sad. "She said the pills might help with your anxiety too, love."

"There's nothing wrong with me," I said, stomping my feet as I walked. "I'm not taking those stupid pills"

"Honey, please... they might help."

"Mum – I'm not going to take them, and you can't make me."

"I'm not going to make you take them," Mum said, looking at Dad, who just stared down at the ground. "But you know that medicine can help sometimes."

"Sure, Mum," I said. "I know medicine can help some people, and that's fine – that's good for them, but it's not what I want."

*I want my dreams – I need them... I need to get back to that magical place where everything is light and beautiful.*

I was tired after talking to the doctor, but I was looking forward to the sleepover.

Ella lived in the suburbs, about ten minutes' drive from town. Mum parked the car outside a modern-looking house.

"I'm coming inside to meet the parents first," she insisted.

"Fine," I said, and got out of the car.

Ella's dad answered the door. He was skinny and balding with glasses and looked nothing like Ella.

"Awa!"

Ella hugged me. She showed me around while our parents talked.

"Your house is so big," I said, thinking of our small apartment, "and fancy!"

"It has to be big because there are five of us here," Ella said. She showed me the TV room where her two older brothers were watching cartoons.

"Hi," I said. They barely looked at me, one of them grunted.

"Teenagers!" Ella said. "Anyway, we are going to

order pizza and watch movies up in my room, and eat ice cream!"

"Sounds great," I said, and it was.

We watched movies on Ella's bed. The walls of her room were painted yellow, and she had an enormous teddy-bear collection, which she seemed a bit embarrassed of. I liked the soft toys, and I was a little bit jealous that Ella's room – and whole house – was so big. She didn't seem to notice. She just kept talking about Evan and how much she liked him.

"Why don't you just call him?" I said. "Tell him how you feel. It will be better than thinking about it so much."

"What if he doesn't feel the same way though," Ella said.

"At least you'll know," I said, "which is usually better than not knowing."

Ella sighed. "Okay, I'll call him after dinner."

When the pizza arrived, I asked Ella if they had any hot sauce in the house. They happened to have my favourite kind. Ella's eyes widened as I poured it over my slice of cheese pizza.

"How the heck can you eat that?" She asked.

"It's a thing me and my dad do," I told her. "He got me used to hot sauce when I was a baby because he was worried he would have to eat bland food, and he can't handle that because his mum was such a good cook."

"A spicy cook?" Ella said, and laughed.

"Yeah, I guess... she was Chinese."

"What part of China did your dad's family come from?" Ella asked.

"The weird thing is, I don't even know. Dad doesn't talk about his family much. His Mum's family has been in New Zealand for generations though – since the gold rush – so that's more than a hundred years, I think. His dad was Scottish. He came over to New Zealand after the Second World War. Dad told me his parents were market gardeners, but they died when he was a teenager."

That was it – everything I knew about Dad's family in a few sentences.

"Makes sense," Ella said. "Are you going to pour hot sauce over your ice cream too?"

"I've never tried that," I said.

"I dare you!" said Ella.

So when it came time to eat ice cream, I poured hot sauce over one spoonful, just to see the look on Ella's face. I took a bite of the cold-hot dessert and watched her gulp.

"It's actually pretty good!" I said and poured more over the rest of my bowl.

"Oh my gosh!" Ella said.

After we had eaten, Ella got up the courage to call Evan, even though he just lived across the street.

"Do you want me to leave the room?" I asked.

"No! Stay!" Ella said. "I need the moral support."

"Okay…"

I sat awkwardly on the end of her bed while she started the conversation.

"Hey, Evan. What are you up to? Nothing much? Oh, I'm just here with Awa, yeah, we just had pizza and ice cream – you will not believe what Awa did, she had hot sauce on her ice cream! I know! She said it was really good! What's *that?*... Oh, you can tell me. Oh..."

I saw Ella's face fall.

"Oh, really? Wow... Okay. I don't know if you should tell her. I better go now. See ya."

Ella threw her phone down on the bed and collapsed beside me.

"What's wrong?" I asked. "Did you tell him?" I could see she was crying.

"I didn't get a chance," Ella said. "He told me he likes *you!*"

*Awkward.*

I didn't know what to say. Ella was so upset, and I didn't know how to make it better.

"I'll write him a letter," I said. "I'll explain that I don't feel that way about him."

"You don't have to do that," Ella said, wiping her eyes.

"Isn't it better that he knows?" I asked.

"It might hurt his feelings," she said.

I looked at Ella. "I can tell you care a lot about him, but this is just weird for me."

"Okay," she said, "but are you sure, you don't like him back? He's pretty cute."

I yawned and thought about Evan with his messy black hair; he looked a bit like a younger version of my dad, which wasn't really appealing. "Yep, pretty sure."

"Well, that's a relief." Ella said. "Hey, it's getting quite late. We should probably get some sleep."

We set up our blankets and pillows on Ella's big bed and got ready to go to sleep.

I listened to Ella snoring softly beside me and felt glad to have such a nice friend, especially when everything else in my life was so crazy.

I was afraid of doing something embarrassing like talking in my sleep, but I was also excited to see Veila again and to see if I could go back to the Grove.

*I am water, earth, sun and sky...*

I finished the charm, hoping I got all the words right, but nothing seemed to happen. I tried again and again...

*Nothing.*

Eventually, I drifted off to sleep anyway and had strange, blurry dreams about the old house again.

CHAPTER ELEVEN

*I* was disappointed and tired the next morning... *why didn't the charm work? Did I get the words wrong? What if I can never make it back there?*

I didn't talk to Ella much because I was lost in my own thoughts, but after I got home, I did what I said I would do; I wrote a note to Evan, telling him that I only liked him as a friend and nothing more. I put it into my school bag. It seemed innocent enough. I had no idea how much trouble that little piece of paper was going to cause me.

Mum kept asking me how I was feeling after talking to Dr Spancer, but I didn't want to talk about it.

I was still tired from not getting much sleep the night before and I was excited about the possibility of more amazing dreams, so I decided to have a nap. I tried to repeat the charm Veila had given me again, but instead of arriving in the Grove, I was in front of the old house again.

I heard the hissing of the snake and began to run through the forest–faster and faster. The snake was quicker than me. I could feel its breath on the back of my neck, sense its jaw opening wide. I screamed – waking myself up.

*The charm didn't work.*

Maybe I was just too tired to dream well, with everything going on in my waking life.

That night, I couldn't sleep. I kept thinking about Ella and Evan, and about Melody, and about Dr Spancer. I really wanted to get back to the meadow and the Grove and to talk to Veila again, but I was also still freaked out by the nightmare about the snake chasing me. I kept the light on even though Mum nagged me to turn it off.

I tried repeating the charm, over and over, but I was still awake.

"I am water, earth, sun, and sky…"

I felt stupid.

I got up to go to the bathroom. The apartment was lighter than usual. I went to the window to see a full moon rising in the sky. Moonlight was flooding in.

*Maybe that's why I can't sleep.*

I went back to my room to lie down.

I held my hands up in the moonlight and looked at my index fingernail. I could almost see a faint glimmer, but maybe it was just my imagination.

Eventually, I relaxed and drifted off. I was walking down a path… the path towards the Grove.

*Yes!*

I got to the circle of trees.

*Wow.*

It was even more beautiful than last time... and different somehow.

The stream looked wider than before; the plants looked even more lush and vibrant, and...

I looked down at a small shrub, *kawakawa?*

"But how could it be here?" I wondered, aloud.

"You must have brought it here," Veila's voice said. "What does it mean to you?"

"This grows in Nannie's garden in Kāwhia," I said. The plant reminded me of her and my great-aunt Rosetta, and of how much I missed them. They always drank tea from the kawakawa leaves that she said cured just about everything.

"So it's ancestral," Veila said. "Interesting..."

"What do you mean?" I asked.

"It could be a warning," Veila said. "Or it could be some other kind of message."

"How can I tell?"

"Warnings will fade quickly," Veila said, "because the danger will become obvious."

*Danger,* I wondered, *what kind of danger could I be in?*

"But..." Veila continued, "other kinds of messages from the ancestors tend to last a lot longer."

"Do you mean the ancestors are actually out there somewhere, and they're talking to me through this plant?" I asked.

"Yes," said Veila.

I looked up to see her, hovering above the pond,

and suddenly remembered my earlier frustrations. "I've been trying to get back here, but your charm didn't work!"

"You're here, aren't you?" Veila asked, coming closer to me.

"But I tried it lots of times, and…"

"I didn't say it would be easy," Veila said, splashing through the water, sending prisms of rainbow light around the Grove.

"No, but you said…"

"Did you do the breathing thing?" she asked.

"What breathing… oh…" *That's right; there was something else, something before the words.* "I forgot."

"That's the most important part," Veila said, splashing me and giggling.

I wiped the refreshing drops away.

"I was too busy focusing on trying to remember the words," I said.

"You humans are always doing that, as far as I can tell."

"Doing what?" I asked.

"Thinking too much," she said. "Worrying too much to pay attention."

"But I *was* paying attention," I said.

"Not to the most important part."

"So that's the most important part?" I asked. "Breathing?!"

"You have to be centred," Veila said.

"What do you mean?"

"Centred as in… focused in the present… centred in

yourself."

"I thought it was a bad thing to be self-centred." I laughed, and the sound seemed to echo in colourful patterns across the trees surrounding the Grove.

"That's very odd," Veila said. "What else is supposed to be at the centre of *you*?"

"Other people, I guess, or more important things like saving the planet."

"But how..." Veila said, "can you really do anything if you are not centred in yourself?"

"I... I don't know," I said, my shoulders slumping. I was sick of arguing and ready to listen.

I practiced the breathing, slowly... counting to four as I breathed in, and then to six as I breathed out.

After a while I opened my eyes and looked around. Veila was sitting on a boulder, watching me, curiously.

"Breathing is boring!" I said.

"Exactly!" said Veila.

"What?"

"You need to bore your thinking-brain into going to sleep so that you can really be present," she replied. "and you also need to make sure you are in the dark."

"What?" I said. "Do you mean I need to sleep with the light off?"

"Of course," Veila said. "You need to spend time in the dark – in the void. That is where all new things come from."

"What are you talking about?" I said, crossing my arms.

"The charm will work better in the dark," Veila said.

"So if you want to come back here, you better follow my instructions."

"Okay, whatever," I said. It didn't really make sense, but it was worth a try to get back to this amazing place.

I lay in the soft grass, surrounded by bright orange and blue wildflowers that smelled like caramel and looked up at the purple, swirling sky.

I sighed, it felt so good just to be there, after the past few days of stress.

"It's so beautiful here," I said. "I think... right now, this is the best part of my life."

"Really?" Veila sounded curious.

"Everything else is kind of a mess," I said. "But it sounds pretty sad, doesn't it, that my dreams are better than my real life?"

"You *still* keep thinking they aren't real life?" Veila asked.

"This can't be real," I said. "It's too good... it's impossible."

I woke up to the sound of rain. I lay in bed wondering...*did saying it was impossible take me out of the dream?*

*Do I have to believe in it, for it to be real... or would that just make me insane?*

# CHAPTER TWELVE

*I*t was a really boring long weekend, and I was also dreading going back to school and having to face Evan. I wondered if I could just avoid him altogether. Mum and Dad had both been trying to talk to me about Dr Spancer. I *hated* that they thought something was wrong with me. Dad called, and I told him I was busy even though I wasn't. I just wanted to get away from both my parents and away from my life – at least from my waking life.

I tried the charm again that night. This time I followed Veila's instructions. I relaxed properly. I turned off the light and faced my own dark bedroom. My mind raced with fears of monsters, snakes, demons, but I got into bed and focused on my breathing.

I counted to slow my breaths the way Veila had shown me – four on the in-breath, six on the out-breath. It was quite relaxing. I decided I was ready to try the charm.

*I am water, earth, sun, and sky.*
*I am dawn, noon, dusk and midnight.*
*I am the whisper in the wind...*
*... and I am here.*

I was in the Grove. I could tell by the uplifting feeling and the swishing sound of the stream. This time the air smelled like vanilla in the warm sun. The kawakawa shrub still glistened in front of me – so maybe it wasn't a warning, but some kind of message. *What does it mean?*

I had googled it the day before to try to solve the mystery, but all I'd found was how it was used to treat cuts and itchy bites and digestive issues, and even to bless things like food, births, and deaths... *so versatile... but what does it mean here, for me?*

I relaxed onto the spongy grass and let my eyes soak up the dazzling wonder of the Grove. I felt so... at home – much more here than I ever did when I was awake.

I couldn't see Veila. I called out to her, but no one came, so I played by myself in the Grove. I watched a beautiful lotus unfold in the pond, blossoming in rainbow colours right before my eyes! I splashed in the stream, which seemed to be somehow bigger than it was last time. I could have sworn I saw a pink glimmer of something in the water, but it vanished as quickly as it had appeared.

I lay in the grass, looking at the beautiful sky that swirled in so many shades of purple. I practiced doing backflips – which is pretty good when you can kind of fly, but I didn't fly up too high. Something told me it was safer on the ground.

I noticed bright pink berries growing in little bushes around the Grove – I wondered if they were safe – they smelled delicious like Nannie's blackberry crumble. They tasted amazing: a combination of pancakes with maple syrup, berry cordial and cinnamon donuts all put together! The flavour seemed to flow right through my body, making me stronger somehow, and more energized.

After a while, I decided to explore. I followed a path out of the Grove, through the forest, into wide-open fields. I was back in the meadow; only it had changed again. This time there was a large lime-green cube sitting right in the middle of the grass, wobbling a little in the sunlight. Veila was coming towards me.

"There you are!" I said.

"Yes," she replied, "and there you are… good. We have work to do."

"What do you mean?" I asked.

"We will start with something simple," Veila gestured towards the cube.

"Where did you get that?" I asked. "And what is it?"

"I arranged it," said Veila.

"It looks like a massive chunk of lime jelly," I said.

Veila beamed proudly at me.

"I wanted to ask you something," I said. "You know how you said I was special or something... a sensitive. What does that really mean?"

"It means there's work to do," Veila said, gesturing to the enormous jelly cube.

I laughed, looking at the strange fantastical landscape around me. "When I think of work, I think of office buildings like where my parents work," I said. "I couldn't imagine anything like that here."

"Work is what you make of it," Veila said.

"Who is the boss?" I asked.

"Boss?" Veila asked. "What's a boss?"

"Who's in charge?"

She gave me a blank look. Eventually, she replied: "We are all charged with what we can do and what we must do."

"And..."

"And," said Veila, "this is the first part of your training."

"Really?" I said. "You're training me with jelly?"

"Of course I am," Veila said. "You need to learn to shape things – to move through different textures and atmospheres if you want to help with the dreamwork."

"I still have no idea what that means," I said. "But okay, whatever..."

Veila instructed me to try to move through the giant cube of jelly, in any way that I could. It was hard work. The jelly both smelled and tasted like lime! It felt like hours of trying to wriggle through such a big surface area, and once I got inside, it was even harder.

"I've had enough," I said. Pulling myself out and panting on the soft spongy grass as I tried to wipe the excess jelly off.

"That's enough for one day," said Veila, and turned, as if to go.

"Wait!" I said. "I still don't know what I'm doing here."

"You're sitting in the meadow," Veila responded.

"I mean – here," I gestured around. "What's the point... why am I doing this in my dream?"

"Oh – that's easy," Veila said. "You're alchemizing..."

"What do you mean alchemizing?"

"You're bringing things together – reconnecting the fragments that have splintered off from the whole... unifying... or at least you are learning how to."

"I don't understand what any of those things are, or how to ... or why," I said, resting my head in my hands.

"Come with me; I want you to meet someone."

Veila led me towards the far edge of the meadow where another magnificent tree stood, even taller than the Elisiad tree.

Its branches stretched up so far towards the sky that I couldn't see how high they went. Its bark was gnarled and twisted in tones of brown and red and gold.

"It's beautiful!" I said, I'd never seen such a gorgeous tree. *How had I never noticed it before?*

"Meet the Priestess Tree," said Veila.

"What does that mean?" I asked.

"Come here," Veila said, leading me closer to the tree. "Put your hand up and listen!"

I put my hand up towards the bark, tentatively, not knowing what other surprises this strange place might have in store.

There was a warm, pleasant sensation on my palm, followed by a slight tingling that ran up through my arm, through my body. It almost felt like sound but on the inside. I closed my eyes.

"That's right," Veila said, relax and let her take you on a journey.

I felt as if I was being called down into the earth, but it wasn't a bad feeling. I felt strong and stable, bolstered by the power of the Priestess Tree.

I let my mind wander down through the layers of earth until I saw her, the Priestess under the tree, her hair connected to the root system, her arms narrow, her belly rounded, her body connected with the earth, her eyes closed as if in meditation.

"Ask her," Veila said. "Ask her to show you why you're here."

"Show me... please," I whispered.

The Priestess opened her hazel coloured eyes. A circle formed in front of her belly, inside I saw a handful of smooth stones, a stormy sea, a bird sweeping over, I felt a sense of freedom, but I didn't quite understand...

"What does it mean?" I asked.

*Listen,* a voice echoed back, deep and rich as the

earth.

I looked again, my mind ran with a sudden stream of ideas – I noticed circle was an oval, like an egg shape – eggs mean new life, so maybe this is my new life? The anchor is about grounding – stopping, pausing, standing still. The bird is freedom...

As soon as I'd had those thoughts, the image disappeared to be replaced by a peaceful glowing image of a woman who was also a star, looking down on the earth.

*You are a light – a light to guide others – a sensitive child who can connect to the meaning of everything and bring it back to the dark world.*

"The dark world?" I wondered aloud

*The world you call 'home' the world you think is 'real'.*

I realised the images and thoughts I was having were actually coming from the Priestess.

*The dark world which has splintered like broken glass and let all the meaning leak out through the cracks.*

"How can I fix this?" I asked. "How can I possibly do anything? I know nothing."

The image transformed again to show the sedimentary layers of the earth, dark winding caves... then the image shifted to above-ground; the sky... a dark-haired girl riding on the back of a giant bird, over cliffs and out to sea. *You just need to trust the process and be brave. Continue the journey, find the sea cliffs, find the gulls, soar, be free.*

"Well, that was confusing," I said to Veila, and promptly woke up.

# CHAPTER THIRTEEN

The next day I finally got a call from Melody, apologising for what she had said in our fight.

"It's okay," I said, but my words felt hollow. I knew we were just too different to keep being best friends.

I went to sleep that night in my dark bedroom, reciting Veila's charm again. I arrived smoothly from my waking state into my dream, in the delightful blossomy sunshine of the Grove. *Yes! It worked again*!

Veila was there, waiting for me.

"It's about time you got here."

"Why?" I asked my small shining friend, who was darting about over the rocks by the pond.

"It's time you learned more about the realm if you're going to help with Dreamwork."

"I still don't know what Dreamwork is," I said, although I was excited by the prospect of exploring the Dreamrealm.

"All in good time," Veila said. "Can you fly?"

"Yes." I thought back to the dream I had of the carnival, and how I kind of just bounced really high, up into the air. "I think I remember…"

I crouched down and prepared myself to jump.

"Not here!" Veila said, with concern in her tone. "The Grove is sacred – it's protected space – we enter and exit by the paths."

"Okay."

Veila was being strangely formal for a dream creature.

We walked out of the Grove, down the green path made of stones and through the dense forest, glimmering with the mysterious lights that I knew were glowing fungi.

Once we reached the edge of the meadow, Veila paused.

"This place is as good as any," she said.

"Okay," I went through the process of preparing to jump, but willed myself to go much further, then I took off. I was rising, higher and higher; butterflies fluttered in my tummy like ones I could see over the trees. I focused out, towards the meadow, forward, I was moving upwards still, hundreds of meters in the air. I could see more of the swirling purple sky, stretching out on all sides. So much more of the landscape was visible, all around me into the distance.

I could see the Priestess Tree and the Elisiad tree further behind, towards the forest that continued for miles. I could see mountains in the distance with snowy white peaks, and what looked like a desert.

"It's an island!" I said, realising it as I spoke the words.

"Of course," said Veila. "Keep flying!"

I caught a glimpse of a big body of water before I started to sink down again. "It's still more like a big jump than flying," I said to Veila, as I landed back on the ground.

"Bounce again!" Veila called out. "Before you lose momentum."

I prepared myself to bounce again, and this time, I really took off.

"This is much more like flying!" I called to Veila, over my shoulder.

"Yes – you just have to lean in the direction where you want to go."

"It's working!"

"So where do you want to go?"

"Is that a lake over there?" I asked, pointing to the large expanse of purple water, visible in the distance, along the edge of the forest.

"Yes," said Veila. "It's the Lake of Reflections."

"Can we go there?" I asked. "I love lakes." They reminded me of happy memories of our family holidays to lake Taupo when I was a little kid.

"Okay – just lean that way, and let's go!"

It was easier said than done. I kept getting distracted by different parts of the landscape which pulled me off in various directions. Colours and shapes flashed in the corner of my eye but then disappeared when I tried to look at them. Patterns flickered and transformed across the surface of the water changing as I looked at them as if they were responding to my gaze.

"Focus," Veila said. "Or we'll never get there!"

I focused on the lake, its sparkling surface reflecting the purple of the sky. As we came into land, I was struck by how stunningly beautiful it was. I landed on its shores and looked out. The lake was smooth and flat apart from one island near the centre. The water's surface swirled along with the sky above. I felt calm and reassured, just looking at it.

Veila floated next to me.

"Can we swim in it?" I asked her.

"*You* probably can," Veila said. "I don't swim. It's not my medium."

"Is it safe?"

"I expect so," Veila replied. "Just keep your mind in a good place."

I moved to the edge of the water. I looked down to where my feet should be and imagined them into being there.

I walked closer, to dip my toes into the shiny violet lake.

"It's not cold," I said to Veila. "I think it's the same temperature as me."

I could barely feel the water around my toes, but when I stepped further into the water, I felt a reassuring calmness. I wasn't sure if it was the effect of the water or if it was just the loveliness of the shimmering lake, that stretched out all around me. I walked out and then dove in. It was delightful, soothing… and somehow energising, too.

"This is great!" I called to Veila. "Are you sure you can't come in?"

"It's not my medium," Veila repeated.

"Okay, suit yourself." I swam out, deeper into the lake. I floated on my back, feeling all the worries about school and home slip away. I tried splashing at the water. The droplets rose up to make rainbows in the air.

"Awesome!"

I swam out, even further, looking towards the island in the distance, scanning around the shore. Half of the lake was surrounded by forest and the other half, a sandy beach. I wondered what kinds of dream creatures lived around here, or inside the lake, even. The thought was mildly terrifying – but I remembered what Veila had said about being safe here as long as I kept my mind in a good place. I focused on the fun of swimming, being in the lake, splashing, and floating. After a while, I glanced up at the island again. I could have sworn it was closer than the last time I looked.

I paused for a minute, watching.

Yes… it's definitely getting closer!

I called out to Veila, "Come here!"

"I told you, I can't."

I swam back towards her.

"Is it just me, or is that island closer than it was?"

"Island?"

"Yes – that island."

Veila giggled.

"What?"

"You think it's an island!"

I looked more closely; it certainly looked like an island, a smallish one, about the size of a truck, with not much growing on it. I was suddenly horrified.

"Is it a creature?" My imagination raced with thoughts of lake monsters.

"Stop that!" Veila said. "Look, you're messing up the lake."

All around me, the water was choppy.

"It reacts to your feelings – that's why I told you to keep your mind in a good state."

"Veila – what is that thing? Is it safe?" I asked, calming down because Veila was clearly not worried. I noticed the lake calmed too.

"Of course, it is. You don't think I'd let you come out here to be eaten by a lake dragon or something?"

I relaxed a bit, wondering what kind of creature it was – so large and rocky.

"He's coming to say hello!"

"What?!" I asked.

The water around me started to move in a surprising way, just as the island creature began to rise from the lake, expanding in size as it did so until it was more like the size of a large house!

I trembled in terror at being in front of such a massive creature.

"Hello?" I said, tentatively.

"Many greetings."

The voice that responded sounded ancient and wizened. It spoke from what could have been a rocky outcropping, but which I realised was a head, connected to the front of the island in a shape familiar to me.

"A turtle!" I could see it now, what I had previously thought to be an island was just the topmost part of the turtle's shell.

"Amazing!" I said.

The turtle's chuckle was deep and resonant. It sent little ripples out across the lake's surface.

"Here you are – at last," the turtle said, in his low, slow voice. "I am Honu, the guardian of the lake... and I have been waiting a long time for a *Dreamweaver* to come."

"Dreamweaver?" I asked. "I thought that was what Veila is."

"Oh, goodness, no!" Veila said. "My job is the dreamcharming. It's just a small part of the dreamweaving."

"But you never said I was a Dreamweaver," I said to Veila.

"I didn't know for sure, until now. I just knew you were a sensitive – but Awa – this is… this is big! I don't even know how to explain it. We've been looking for a Dreamweaver for so long!"

"So, there's supposed to be just one?"

"Not supposed to be – it's just that they are so uncommon," said Veila.

"Not many do this work. Not many can," Honu said. "Every human who dreams is playing their part in the evolution of all that is... but much of the work you must do is in the dark."

"What?" I said it was a bit much to follow.

"Many thousands of years ago, the planet had no flowers, and then there was one – one flower, followed by another and another – and so it is with Dreamweavers. We have only seen one before you, and now we have another, and soon, we will have many more... we need you – all of you, to do the work of expanding consciousness – the evolving – we are all becoming..."

"Becoming what?" I asked. This was way too cryptic for me.

Honu kept talking as if he hadn't heard me "– but so few can walk in both worlds and do the work consciously. Some can dream consciously, but very few move beyond the rooms of the mind."

It was great to finally be getting some answers. I just wish I could understand what they meant.

"So this has to do with what you called me before, a 'sensitive'?" I asked Veila.

"Yes – that is a factor. Sensitives are much more able to feel their way through the dreamscapes. It helps."

"And what does a Dreamweaver do?" I asked, looking at Honu and then at Veila.

Veila spun around in the air "So, so many things! But the main work is to find the fragments and reconnect them."

"The fragments like the one on the throne that insisted I was special?" I asked.

"That sort of thing, yes, and to keep the Shadow at bay."

"The Shadow?" I felt a shiver run down my spine.

"The Shadow grows in denial, the more you humans cannot face your uncomfortable aspects, and project them outside yourselves, the greater the Shadow grows."

"What does all that have to do with the fragments?" I asked.

"The fragments are aspects of the Shadow, whether they know it or not... like small shards of a broken mirror. They are disconnects in our world, reflecting the greater disconnect of the Shadow itself."

It was all too much to think about. The words swirled around in my mind... *fragments, shards... disconnect... Shadow.*

I shivered again – it was a similar feeling to just before when Honu had emerged from the lake – so enormous that it triggered awe and shock and terror. The lake around me swirled with my own confusion, and I saw that Honu had also started to slowly glide away.

"It is good to meet you, Dreamweaver. You have much to learn and much work to do – so I will not keep you, but you may return to visit me," and with that, Honu dropped down into the water again.

I swam back to the shore, feeling terrified.

"What's wrong?" Veila asked me as we walked back up.

"I'm – well, it's all quite a lot to take in… also, my parents are worried about my mind. They are making me talk to a psychiatrist."

"A sci-kia-what?" Veila asked.

"A brain doctor," I looked down, only to see I had no feet again.

"Oh – you're fine," Veila assured me.

# CHAPTER FOURTEEN

*I* was holding the note to Evan, but I didn't know how to give it to him.

*I could pass it to him right before class started, so I don't have to talk to him, but then he might feel bad in class.*

I decided to wait until just before lunchtime, but I was still holding the note in my hand as I walked into the classroom.

Just as I was about to sit down at my desk, I felt the note being pulled out from between my fingers.

"What?!" I looked up to see Felicity.

"What do we have here?" she asked.

"Give that back!" I yelled and reached up for it. Felicity skipped across to the other side of the room.

"Oooh," she called out. "Awa and Evan, up a tree!" I looked around to see Ella walk in.

Felicity lowered her voice. "I guess it makes sense since you're both Asians."

I glared at her.

"Just wait until the whole school finds out!" she shrieked and ran out of the classroom.

"No!" I chased Felicity out into the hallway, grateful that Mr Jasper wasn't there yet, because he would probably have yelled at me to sit down. Then again, Felicity wouldn't have been so loud if a teacher was watching.

"Give that back!" I called out to her, but she disappeared into the girls' bathrooms. I gave up following her. *What's the point? That's probably just what she's wanting.*

I went back to class and sat awkwardly, while Mr Jasper called the role, trying to get Ella to look at me so I could mouth, "Sorry."

Ella seemed to be avoiding me. *Great... just great.*

Things only got worse at morning break. I went to the bathrooms, and my gut sank to the floor. It was everywhere: "Awa and Evan" in love hearts scrawled on the mirror and walls in pink lipstick.

I felt sick.

I grabbed a paper towel and began wiping it off. The paper towels looked like they were covered in blood. The rubbish bin was like a murder had been committed by the time I finished.

The mirror and walls were smudged, but at least there was nothing with our names anymore. No one else would see what Felicity had written, but I knew a bunch of people would have seen it before I had even got there.

As I stepped out of the bathroom, trying to rub the

last of the lipstick off my hands, Felicity snapped a picture of me. *Probably just to show all her friends how upset I am.* At least that's what I thought at the time.

*This day is turning into hell!*

I didn't manage to find Ella alone until after the bell rang for the end of the day. I saw her waiting to be picked up by the school gate

"I'm so sorry!" I said. "I was trying to make it better, but I only made it worse. Ella was crying again.

"I don't believe you," she said. "I think you like him back, and you were just being nice to me."

"No," I said. "Honestly."

"It's okay," she said. "You two can't help the way you feel. Why don't you just admit it, and you can go out with Evan and leave me alone!"

"Ella," I said. "I know you don't believe me, but I have to tell you something." I looked down.

"What?" she asked.

"I don't know if there's something wrong with me..." I said. "I've never told anyone this."

She looked up at me, curious.

"I've never liked anyone that way – ever. I've never had a crush at all."

Ella was quiet for a while.

"Never?" she asked

"No," I said.

"Oh," she said. We stood there, awkwardly, watching cars drive past.

"Maybe one day you will," she said.

"Maybe," I replied. "But you can guarantee I don't like Evan!"

I might have said that too loud. Ella's eyes widened. She was looking behind me. I turned to see...

"Evan!"

His face looked pale, upset, he turned and ran away.

"Oh damn," I said, smacking my face with my hands, *now I've hurt two friends in the same day! What is wrong with me!*

I walked home feeling way too many emotions all at once.

I was guilty and sad about Evan being upset, but it actually felt quite good to tell Ella *one* of my secrets.

I didn't know if she believed me, and I knew I couldn't tell her about my dreams.

As I walked, I felt worse and worse. The anxiety started building in my chest; everything went grey, and the thoughts circled in my head.

*Ella won't believe me. She'll think I'm a liar, and so will Evan. They will both hate me. I will have no friends. Felicity will start rumours about me, and everyone will tease me and laugh at me. There's something seriously wrong with me, and I don't even know how bad it is yet.*

I felt my phone buzzing in my pocket, but I didn't want to answer it. It was probably just Mum anyway.

By the time I got home, I was crying and breathing too fast, and I couldn't seem to stop.

"Awa!" someone called out, just as I was about to go into our building. I turned around.

"Ella?"

Ella was there, holding a tub of ice-cream and a bottle of hot sauce.

"I saw the look on your face, when you left," Ella said. "I wanted to cheer you up. I got my dad to take me to the shop, and he said he can pick me up in an hour."

"What about Evan?" I asked.

"It's okay," Ella said. "I'll talk to him."

"Thanks," I said, letting her into the building. "How did you even know where I live?"

"You told me which building you were in. I was hoping you would answer your phone eventually."

I remembered my phone buzzing earlier. "Oh yeah, sorry for not answering."

"You don't have to apologise," Ella said. "I'm the one who should be sorry. You were really caught in the middle of all this, and it wasn't your fault."

We made big bowls of ice cream, and I put hot sauce on mine again, just for fun, and because it's actually quite good.

"I hope Evan is okay," I said. "Felicity can be such a nasty piece of work!"

"Yeah, at least everyone knows *that*." Ella said. "I'll call Evan later."

"And maybe this time, you can tell him how you really feel," I suggested.

"Maybe," Ella said, "or maybe I'll wait a while, until he's feeling better."

"Thanks," I said. "I hate that I hurt his feelings."

"You didn't mean to," Ella said. "You're a good

person… actually, I have something for you. Give me your hand."

I held my hand out, and Ella dropped something into my palm. It was small and silver – a chain with a single star charm.

"It's a friendship bracelet," Ella said, holding out her hand to reveal a glint of silver next to her teddy-bear watch. "I have a matching one, see. I was going to give it to you before when we had the sleepover, but I forgot."

I smiled. "Thank you," I said. "I love it."

"The thing is," Ella continued, "it's like I said before – I didn't really have any friends, before you came along, apart from Evan. And I'm glad you're strong enough to stand up to Felicity. I'm sorry I doubted you – you really are a good person."

I smiled and hugged my friend… even after such a terrible day, things didn't seem so bad now.

I arrived in the Dreamrealm that night to find Veila relaxing on a bounder by the stream. Just being there instantly made me relax, and all my worries seemed to drift away in a cloud of colourful butterflies. I sighed.

"Hi," I said. "I've meant to ask you… what is a splinter, or a fragment or whatever they are called?"

I sat on a rock dangling my feet into the water of the stream. Veila floated in the air next to me.

"A splinter, or a fragment?"

"How can you not know these things?" I asked Veila. "Isn't it your job to know?"

"My job?" Veila asked. "Then what is your job?"

I shrugged. "To go to school I guess, although I wish it was to play video games and watch videos and read."

"What's a video game?" Veila asked.

I tried to explain it to her – how it was this thing on a screen that you tried to influence and that they usually got harder and harder...

"But why would you want it to get harder?" Veila said. "Why would you like it, if it was hard?"

"Because easy is boring," I said.

Veila smiled and spun around in the air. "The thing with me is that I can only know the things I need to know right now... in any particular now. This is how it is with dreamcharmers, we can only contain what we need, so when we are working with the dreaming humans, all we know is what we need to say. We don't know why, or how."

"So if that's your job – helping people to evolve through giving them dream suggestions, or whatever it is you do..." I said. "... Why are you here with me?"

Veila looked at me, curiously "because I've never met a Dreamweaver before and because it's nice."

"What's nice?" I asked.

"Spending time with you," Veila said.

"Like a friend?"

"I've never had a friend."

"Well, now you do," I said and smiled at her.

Veila floated down and sat on the boulder, beside

me. We looked out at the big friendly trees around the Grove; they seemed to breathe with us.

"So, what is it you wanted to know about?" she asked. "I will see if I can help you."

"I want to understand all this better," I said, gesturing around me. "I get all these ideas – see all these connections, and sometimes I'm wrong."

I told Veila about the snake dreams and about thinking Evan's uncle was evil when, really, he was nice.

"Fear distorts things," Veila said, sounding very wise. "And you know snakes… snakes are a symbol of power, and not all power is bad."

"I interesting…" I said. "You know, fragments, remember… like the one we saw in that room?"

"What room?" Veila asked.

"The room in the domed building, the Rooms of Mind."

"Hmm, it could have been anything in there."

"Yes, but you said… there was this little figure sitting on a throne on top of a pile of mattresses saying they were special, and you said that was a splinter – like a part of something bigger that had splintered off, a fragment."

"Oh, yes… of course!" Veila said. "Why?"

"Well," I looked at Veila's small peachy-glowing figure, as she floated next to me. "Are they all like that?"

"No," Veila replied simply.

"What did they splinter off from? And why? And

what do they have to do with me and with being a Dreamweaver?"

"Those are all very good questions," Veila said.

I sighed. "Really?"

"Yes," Veila said, beaming at me.

"Can't you… isn't there a way I can find out more, now?"

"Of course there is," Veila said. "Let's go!"

"She pulled me by the hand, and I felt a tingle as if a thousand tiny bells were ringing through my skin.

"Where are we going?" I asked.

"To find some fragments for you to see," Veila said.

I followed Veila out of the Grove and into the meadow. She moved so fast that it took me a while to notice I wasn't walking. I was gliding. It felt like a kind of video game. Veila seemed to go faster and faster; my stomach lurched as I accelerated behind her, trying to keep up. I felt fear creeping in, but I wasn't sure if it was to do with moving so fast or whether I was scared of meeting other fragments. The one I had met before was very strange, but it didn't seem dangerous. I had a gut feeling that some of the others might be.

We went past the Priestess Tree and the Rooms of Mind, and then we turned and went further back into the meadow.

"What are we doing?" I called to Veila.

"Looking for fragments," she replied.

"There, look!"

"Where?" I asked.

"Look down."

Below us, against the bright green of the meadow was a little man, all red and smoking in rage as if he was a hot element on the stove.

"Who is that?"

"It's the Angry Man, of course," Veila said, veering away from him and out towards the desert. I could see a funny shape against the barren landscape. At first, I thought it was a statue, but as we neared, I could tell it was a girl dressed in pink on top of a plastic-looking golden throne wearing a matching crown.

"Ummm," I said.

"Don't get too close to that one, either," Veila said. "It never ends well."

"What is she, some kind of doll?" I asked.

"She's the Drama Queen," said Veila. I giggled, thinking of Melody, and feeling relieved that I didn't have to deal with all her stressful dramas anymore.

"And look over there, toward the mountains," said Veila.

I could make out a swirling dark blue cloud at their base; as we got closer, I saw a sad-looking woman in the middle of the cloud, sitting with a broken umbrella.

"The Sad Woman," I said. I didn't know how I knew… I just did.

Veila nodded. Then she grabbed my hand, sending little tingles up my arm, and pulled me back towards the meadow.

Veila pointed out to the left. I could see a shape in the distance. It looked like a bundle of rags.

"What is it?" I asked.

"Another fragment," she said.

As we got closer, I realised that what looked like a pile of old rags and rubbish was moving, slowly, swaying side to side as it if was trying to walk. We stopped a few meters away.

"Hello?" I called out.

"Shhhhhh," said Veila. "It might be dangerous."

"It looks like a pile of junk," I said.

"Hrrrrrmmmm…" the sound came from the bundle. It slowly turned around, although it looked like turning took a lot of effort.

"Hrrrmhrrm,"

The noise was coming from a small wrinkly face somewhere near the centre of the pile, with beady eyes, and a tuft of white hair. There was a pungent smell in the air – like too much old-fashioned perfume.

"Riffraff," it said. "I have no business talking to you." It started to turn back around again. And then stopped and looked at me.

"You…" it said, looking at me more closely. "We've been expecting you…"

I felt a shiver run down my spine, as the creature continued to turn away.

"Wait…" I said. "Who are you?"

"Me?" it said. "Can't you tell, from all my finery?"

"What… finery?" I took a step closer. I could see the rags were made up of velvet, furs, and embroidered silk. On closer inspection, they glistened with gemstones.

"What is it?" I whispered to Veila.

"I think this is a hoarder," Veila said. "It clings to things. It collects shiny things and can't bear to let go."

"Don't look too closely, you... you beggar," it said, backing away slowly. "It's all mine!"

I frowned. "But I don't want any of it. It's just junk," I said.

"Junk!" the hoarder said. "What kind of tomfoolery is this?" It scowled at us. "You're just trying to trick me out of my riches."

"No," I said. "Your riches are not really my style."

"Style!" it said. "I always have everything in style... everything. Look at my emeralds, this season's colour!"

I raised my eyebrows and looked at Veila. "I have no idea what I'm supposed to do with this... thing."

"Thing!?" the creature bellowed.

"What do you mean?" Veila asked me.

"You said Dreamweavers are supposed to alchemize the fragments... I don't know what that means or how I'm supposed to do it."

"I don't know either," Veila admitted. "what do you notice about this one?"

"It's just obsessed with stuff," I said, "and it's trying to carry everything around on its back, which means it can hardly walk."

"What would you know?" the fragment said.

"Actually, it reminds me of how I used to be with toys when I was little. I would carry them around with me, everywhere I went. It used to drive Mum and Dad crazy!"

"Fascinating..." Veila said, looking at me.

"What's that?" the hoarder said, staring at my wrist. I looked down to see the glimmer of the bracelet Ella had given me with the star on it. So it had come with me into the dream too, along with my pyjamas apparently!

"It's just my bracelet."

"Lies!" the hoarder said, moving towards me. "It's pretty and shiny, and that means it most definitely belongs to me!"

It tried to lunge at me. I backed away and watched as the big pile of fabric and jewels toppled over. It groaned and heaved, looking quite funny as it was trying to push itself up. Eventually, it managed to roll over.

"I don't think we are going to learn anything more from this one," Veila said. We began walking away.

"Stop! Thief!" the fragment called out as we left.

We moved back across the meadow towards the forest.

"Well, that was weird!" I said to Veila.

"Was it?" she asked.

"Yes... well, for me, it was. I've never seen anything like it!"

I thought about it for a few minutes.

"What's the point in having all that stuff if you can't really enjoy it anyway?" I asked Veila.

"Good question," she replied.

"It was kind of stuck," I said, "like it just had this one idea that it needed shiny stuff, and that was the only thing it cared about."

"That sounds right," Veila said.

"Are they all like that?" I asked. "That first one I met; it was obsessed with being special, like it was stuck saying the same things too... It's kind of scary"

"Not all," Veila said. "I've seen a lot of variety."

"I still don't get it, though," I said. The frustration was starting to build again. "I don't know what I'm doing here. What's the point of all this?"

"What's your obsession with knowing what's going on all the time?" Veila asked. "That's a bit like a fragment, isn't it? Getting stuck on the same thing?"

"No... it's..." I started, then I realised she was right. *Damn!* "But I'm..."

"I was just kidding!" Veila flipped around in circles, laughing hysterically for a while. "You're much more interesting... mostly," she said, after she had settled down a bit.

"Gee, thanks," I replied, but I also knew she had a point.

Veila's expression suddenly became more serious. "That thing the hoarder said... they have been expecting you," Veila said. "Awa you must be careful. Do not leave the Grove without me – it's not safe."

And with that, I woke up.

# CHAPTER FIFTEEN

It had been a long day. The kids at school were awful – teasing me and Evan after Felicity's stupid lipstick prank, and the teachers had been mad about the smears all around the bathroom and had told off the whole class about it when no one came forward.

That night, I arrived in the Grove, relieved to get away from everything in my waking life.

Something strange appeared in the air in front of me – a red ball. On closer inspection it was a lantern, like the kind at the Chinese lantern festival that Dad sometimes took me to.

*A message from the ancestors...* like the kawakawa, that still grew, bright and glossy in the grove a few feet away. I still didn't know what the kawakawa meant, but as the lantern faded to nothing, I felt a chill of fear – *warnings disappear...* I remembered, *it's a warning...*

"Awa..."

I heard the voice calling me. It wasn't Veila, and it wasn't coming from anywhere in the Grove.

"Awa!"

There it was again.

"Who's there?" I called back; *who else here even knows my name?*

More chills ran down my spine but I needed to find out. Ignoring Veila's warnings I left the Grove and walked down through the forest path towards the sound. *Whatever it is, it's trying to lure me out; the Grove is safe and it wants me to be out there somewhere...*

I thought about going back, but not knowing where the voice was coming from would drive me crazy.

I followed the sound of my name out into the meadow. The sky was darker than usual. Something seemed disjointed about the view as if it were put together by puzzle pieces that didn't quite fit. A strong wind blew the grass in all directions, bringing with is a greasy scent. It surprised me... *I've never seen bad weather in the Dreamrealm before.*

"Awa."

My name rang out again in a sing-song voice. I continued to follow the sound out towards the far side of the meadow. I hadn't been out this far before and I was surprised to find rocky cliffs, descending down to the sea. I'd never really looked at the sea here before. It was a dark, inky shade of indigo. The wind whipped it into choppy waves; I was sure it must have looked even more beautiful on a bright still day.

Something clicked in my memory, *sea cliffs.* That

was what the Priestess Tree had showed me. Cliffs like these. I looked around expecting to see some other sign.

Two figures in the distance moved towards me. One from the left and one from the right. I froze, *should I run?* I wondered. I wanted to run, but I needed to know what was going on.

As they got closer, I could tell that one was a woman with high cheek bones and a classically beautiful face, except for her pale, lavender-tinged skin. She was wearing an elaborate dark blue and silvery ball gown that looked old-fashioned – almost as if she had stepped out of a painting. The other was a man, quite tall, with a chiselled jaw, wearing a pinstriped suit.

"What do you want?" I called out. I didn't want them to get much closer.

"You don't belong here, little girl," the woman said.

"Children belong at home," said the man, as if he was giving a speech, "with their parents, where they are safe and loved."

"What is this?" I asked, feeling trapped. I looked at both of them. "What are you?"

"I am in charge around *here*," the woman said.

"*We* are…" the man interrupted. She gave him a stern look.

"This is my kingdom," she continued, "and I decide what goes and what stays." She narrowed her eyes at me. "We heard you are a *Dreamweaver*. We are not impressed with scum like you!"

I shivered.

"Know that you don't want to be here," said the man. His voice sounded friendly, but it didn't feel that way at all. "We've listened. We know you're unhappy with your life and we're here to help."

*Awa,* I heard Veila's voice this time, I looked from the man in the suit who was smiling to the woman who was looking down her nose at me. I could tell they hadn't heard Veila.

*You need to leave,* Veila's voice said, in my head. *It's not safe.*

"You need to leave," the woman said. "Leave the Dreamrealm and never return. Your kind is not welcome here."

I looked around, wondering what the best way to escape would be; there was enough room between them that I could probably make a run for it, but I didn't know how fast they were.

"You're not in charge!" I said. "No one is in charge here."

The woman threw back her head and laughed a high, cold laugh, and the man followed her, although his laugh sounded a lot warmer, as if it was an inside joke that we all knew. *This is my chance; run while they are distracted by their own laughing.* I bolted, as I quickly as I could.

I glanced back to see them following me, close behind, the woman's face in a scowl, the man's face looking... *plastic.* I almost slowed down to take a closer look but I had to get away. I remembered how quickly I had followed Veila that time when we were looking for fragments. *I need to move fast,* I willed myself to glide like that again. It worked!

I knew I was gaining a good lead. I glanced back to see that the man had removed his mask. Behind it was a *snake!*

*No way.*

It was like the snake in my dreams, the one that had chased me, the one I had seen on the tattooed man who turned out to be nice, but this... *this is the opposite,* I realised. *The man seemed so nice a few minutes ago but it was all an act.*

I focused. *I need to fly as fast as I possibly can.* I could see the forest up ahead, and the beginning of the path that led to the Grove. I willed myself to be there as soon as possible, *safe.* I willed it with every fibre of my being. I could tell they were catching up to me; I could hear the hissing of the snake. I closed my eyes and...

*Pop!*

I was back in the Grove.

"What?" I said aloud.

"What?" Veila replied. "Oh! It's you! You're back!"

"How did I get here?!"

"What do you mean?" Veila said. "And why didn't you listen? I told you not to go anywhere without me!"

I explained about hearing the voice – about being called out of the Grove, about the sneering lavender woman in the ball gown and the man in the suit who looked friendly and smiled a lot but had a snake behind his mask. I told Veila about being followed and willing myself to be back in the Grove and then suddenly finding myself here.

"Oh no!"

"What?" I asked. "What just happened?"

"They've found out about you," Veila said. I had never seen her look so serious.

"Who are they? And how... how did I get here?"

"You must have willed yourself here."

"Is that... is that like teleportation?"

"Telly-pour-what-shin?"

"Never mind," I said. "Just tell me who they are."

"Do they... do they know you are a Dreamweaver?"

I nodded.

"No, no, no!" Veila said, her tiny face sinking into a frown. "This is very bad."

"Veila, please tell me!" I said. "Tell me who they are."

"The man you talked about... we call him the Politician."

"What? Why?"

"It's something to do with how he smiles, and wears a mask, and tells people what he thinks they want to hear... everything he says is a lie," Veila said. "Why, what does politician mean where you come from?"

"It's someone who wants to be in charge, like a leader... I guess. But that sounds about right." I thought about what Mum and Dad sometimes said about the politicians they didn't like.

"That's strange," Veila said. "Why would a leader want to be in charge?"

"Never mind that," I said. I didn't have time for her weird questions. I knew it must be getting late. I could wake up any second. Time was slipping away and this felt like the best chance I'd ever had to find out what was going on.

"Veila, he has a snake under that mask – the same snake that was chasing me in my dreams; I'm sure of it."

Veila nodded.

"What is he, and what is the woman supposed to be? Are they fragments?"

"They are a kind of fragment, I guess… they are bigger Shadow particles."

"What does that mean?"

"The woman…" Veila said. "You said she wore a ball gown."

"Yes," I said. "She looked like some kind of old-fashioned painting."

"You've got to watch her."

"Who is she?" I asked again.

"She is Judgement."

"Judgement?"

"Yes, she… she kind of cuts into everything with her mind, judges it to see if it satisfies her."

"Like she's judgmental?" I asked. "Isn't everyone?"

"The thing is…" Veila said, "trees don't judge each other because they don't need to protect themselves from each other." She gestured at the forest surrounding the Grove.

"What are you getting at?"

"People don't judge trees because they don't have the capacity to actively attack them,"

"Okay," I said. "I get it. People are scared of things that could attack us – like snakes, and spiders, and sharks; people often hate them, but not many people hate trees."

"Yes, so judging is about protection," Veila said, "and everyone has a bit of that kind of thing inside them, but it's usually invisible."

"Are you saying she's a part of… people?"

"Well, she has splintered off, but yes."

"I'm so confused!" I said.

"Judgement hurts us all," said Veila, "while intending to protect us."

"Is she evil?"

"What's evil?" Veila asked.

I sighed. "So she's a kind of super-fragment, and she's not evil, but she's after me, and she wants me out of here."

"That's right," Veila said. "The Dreamrealm is not safe for you now. Stay away!"

"But…"

I tried to protest, but it came out as a groan into my pillow. I was back in bed.

*Stay away.*

Veila's words echoed in my head, and they hurt.

# CHAPTER SIXTEEN

*I* rolled over in bed, curling into a little ball. Pain and nausea shot through my whole body, and I started to sweat. Mum thought I might have the flu and said I could stay home from school, but I knew this had nothing to do with a virus and everything to do with being kicked out of the Dream-realm by the dream creature I trusted the most.

*Is this shame?* I wondered. *I used to belong there – I used to be special... and now I feel like a big pile of trash!*

I stayed in bed all day.

*Everything is so messed up, at school, and in my dreams, I need a break!*

Nothing in my life seemed to be working at all. I kept thinking about Ella and Evan how I had hurt them even though I didn't mean too – even though I was trying to help. I kept thinking about Felicity and how mean she was to write that stuff on the mirror. *What's wrong with that girl?* I wondered. I kept thinking about the dreams, about Judgement and the Politician, and how they had tried to attack me.

*Felicity is just like them. She wants to control everything. I can't escape her in my waking life, and now these creeps are taking over my dreams... Even Veila has told me to stay away.*

I kept hearing the same words in my head: *stay away.*

Veila's words cut into me. I wasn't welcome anymore in the only place that felt like home.

*She's doing this to protect me,* I reminded myself. Veila had looked so scared; maybe by going to the Dreamrealm, I was putting her at risk too.

It was about halfway through the day when I realised what I had to do. *Take the pills.*

The tablets from Dr Spancer were still sitting in a drawer in my room. I hadn't taken any of them; I didn't want to, but that seemed to be the only way to do what Veila wanted – to stay away.

That night, I picked up the small brown bottle with the white lid. The plastic was slightly transparent, so I could see the little pills inside. I opened them, surprised to see they were yellow.

*Take one before bed,* the bottle said. *Do not mix with alcohol, may cause drowsiness, avoid operating heavy machinery.*

I laughed, imagining myself drunk and driving a digger.

I spilled one tiny yellow pill onto the palm of my hand, put it on my tongue, and took a big gulp of water. *Done.*

*Goodbye Dreamrealm.*

I didn't bother turning the light off. I just got into bed, trying to hold back the sobs. Eventually, I gave in and had a good cry: *The Dreamrealm is my place... my special place... the only place I feel at home, and now... It doesn't want me anymore.*

I closed my eyes and slowly drifted off to sleep.

I was in the house again – the old house – my house. It was empty, with no furniture. The lights were all on. I felt drowsy. I walked from room to room, but I didn't find anything. I went out into the back garden. The terrain seemed to morph and shift and blur at the edges, and then, everything became clear.

In front of me, sitting on the lawn, was a table, with a bright red checked tablecloth, and a single chair. The table was laid for one, with cutlery and a plate. I could smell a sickly-sweet scent like candy and perfume.

I moved closer. On the plate was a bright pink cake. I sat down on the chair, took the tiny cake fork, and took a bite of the cake.

That was when I realised I was dreaming.

The cake tasted like dust. I spat it back out again, but I could feel thick heavy darkness flooding down my throat. I was sinking deeper into the chair, even as I tried to get out.

A cackle of cold laughter echoed all around me. I grabbed the arms of the chair to push myself up, but cords appeared out of nowhere before I could move away. They wrapped firmly around my wrists, tying my hands down to the arms of the chair.

"No!" I struggled against the ropes, still feeling foggy.

"We did it!"

I turned to look in the direction of the voice; it was the Politician, in a pinstriped gold and blue suit with a bright golden tie, walking towards me, smiling that big fake smile through his face that I knew was just a mask.

"I told you she would fall for it," a familiar cold voice said from behind me. I knew it was Judgement.

"It was a trap," I said.

"Yes," she said. "It was a trap, and you walked right into it, you even took the pills!"

"How do you know about that?" I asked, feeling drowsy. "Have you been watching me?"

I wrestled against the cords, holding me down, but I gave up, feeling too weary to fight.

"Oh, we have our ways," said the Politician.

"What are you going to do?" I asked.

"I..." Judgement started.

"We," the Politician corrected.

"We," Judgement said, "are going to drain your Dreamweaver powers... which will give me – us – control of the Dreamrealm."

"Why?" I asked.

"Things could be so much better around here." The

Politician smiled. "And I'm going to make them better, for all of us."

"I'll be the judge of that," Judgement said. "I know what's acceptable and what isn't, and quite frankly, there is too much that isn't good enough – poor quality."

"Like the trees," the Politician added.

"Filthy, dirty trees!" said Judgement. "Unsightly!"

"We need the trees," I said. "Especially the Priestess Tree."

"That messy creature! She will have to be the first to go," said Judgement.

"No!"

"You just hold tight, my dear," said the Politician. "This won't hurt a bit."

They disappeared for a moment. I struggled to get out of the chair, but my wrists were tied too tightly by the inky coloured rope. The smell of burnt plastic hung in the air, making me cough.

I heard a creaky noise, like the sound of an old door opening and closing. I turned to see Judgement and the Politician pushing a large rectangular object on wheels, towards me. It was covered in what looked like hundreds of buttons and dials, all in dull, murky colours.

"What is that?" I asked.

"Oh, this is a very clever contraption," said Judgement.

"Like nothing you've ever seen before," the Politician added.

"What does it do?" I asked.

"Just you wait!" Judgement said.

The Politician unwound a tube from the machine and fitted what looked like a purple gas mask onto it.

"No," I said, wriggling as much as I could. "No, no. Really, let's try something else. I can help you. I can work with you."

I did not want that thing on my face!

"We have a vision for this land," said the Politician, "and this is your great chance to be part of it!"

"What's your vision?" I asked, trying to stall them.

"This is going to be the best place ever – in history!" the Politician crowed. "We'll have the biggest stadium around with an enormous podium – perfect for making speeches – and massive high-rise buildings – like you've never seen before, and the tallest building will be my office!"

"What rubbish he spouts!" said Judgment. "The most important thing to have is ballrooms, of course – ballrooms and palaces – where there is not even one speck of dirt – not at all!"

"We'll work out the details later," the Politician said.

It was so awful I could barely imagine it. The Dreamrealm was perfect just the way it was – randomness and all. The last thing it needed was to be covered in buildings and ballrooms!

The Politician beamed at me. "Rest assured, little girl, you're going to be an important part of this key moment in history.

"No, I can help you…" I lied. "Really, I love ball-rooms and podiums and…"

"That won't be necessary," Judgement said.

The Politician fitted the mask over my face, blocking out my peripheral vision. Everything blurred so that the world seemed both too close and too far away.

Then my vision adjusted somehow, and I could see, at least partially. I watched as Judgement lowered a lever. The machine shuddered and began to hum. I could smell gasoline and burning eggs. Something was making me very drowsy…

"No!" I called out, struggling against my own exhaustion. "Veila! Help!"

"Your little friends won't be able to help you, my dear," Judgement whispered in my ear. "Look."

She gestured towards the side of the machine; there was a screen. On it, I could just make out the Dream-realm; only the colours seemed to be getting dimmer.

"They will be the first to go." Judgement spun a dial. The machine clinked and clanked, and the screen panned to Veila. She was next to the Priestess Tree, but her light was fading, she could barely hover, her eyes were closing.

"No!" I tried to yell, but my voice was weak.

I couldn't help Veila and Veila couldn't help me. She was next to the Priestess Tree. *Maybe she was there trying to ask a question, because she knew something was wrong.*

I remembered back to the time I had visited the tree

and asked questions only to receive strange cryptic answers: *the sea cliffs, the gulls, magic stones... what good are they now?*

*What happens to me if I can't get back to my life? If I'm stuck here, in this chair forever being sapped of all my energy by these power-hungry creeps!?*

I can't give up. I need to think of something.

*This is my dream; I have the power.* I repeated this over and over again in my head. I remembered what Veila had taught me about centring; I tried the charm to get back to the Grove:

*I am earth, sea, sun and sky...*

I didn't wake up this time... I stayed exactly where I was, only...

"It's slowing down," the Politician said.

"What?" said Judgement. "Get away from it, you fool!"

She pushed the Politician so hard he fell over onto the ground. *It's working. Something I'm doing is slowing the machine down.* I kept repeating the charm in my head and focusing on centring myself.

"No!" Judgement shrieked, and frantically pushed the different buttons and dials. "It was perfectly calibrated! Perfect! What have you done?"

"Nothing!" said the Politician. "I swear I didn't touch a thing."

"Then, it's her!" Judgement said; she turned towards me. I closed my eyes and tried to look weak while continuing to repeat the charm in my head.

*I am...*

*I am...*

"This little creature is stronger than we anticipated," Judgement said. "Who would have thought it from watching her – she seemed such a pathetic weakling at school."

*They were watching me!* The thought gave me the creeps, but I had to keep focusing on the charm.

"We must turn up the machine, to full power," Judgement announced.

"Full power! Are you sure?" the Politician asked.

*No,* my heart raced in panic.

"Imbecile – of course, I'm sure!"

Judgement lowered another lever and another.

"It's working!" the Politician rubbed his hands together in glee. "We are draining her brain, brain drain, drain brain… it rhymes!"

*No,* I was sinking deeper into the quicksand of exhaustion, but I couldn't let them win; *I need to escape!*

I remembered how I had disappeared the last time Judgement, and the Politician chased me, how I was suddenly back in the Grove. I tried to do the same thing again, but I was so tired. I could barely hold myself up in the chair. I slumped over.

*This is it; there's nothing else I can do... this is the end.*

I couldn't think of anything else – any other way out. I was drowning in a lake of my own hopelessness and despair. I rested my chin on my chest. Tears streamed down my face thinking of all the people I would miss: Mum and Dad, Ella and Evan, Veila… even Melody.

*Summon the gulls.*

The thought came from the back of my mind, like a whisper. It reminded me of talking to the Priestess Tree. *The gulls. Was that what she meant? Maybe the images she showed me weren't just metaphors.*

*Gulls!* I called out in my mind. *I need you! Come here now!*

I repeated this over and over. I didn't know what else to do. I had run out of ideas.

I barely had the energy to lift my head, but I could hardly see, anyway.

Everything went black.

*This is it... I can't fight anymore. I give up.*

Overhead came the squawking sounds.

I heard Judgement shriek "What?!"

"Shoo!" said the Politician's voice.

There was banging and crashing and a lot of yelling and squawking all around me. I couldn't see anything, but I could feel something tugging at my wrist, pulling at the mask.

I slumped out of the chair and onto the ground. *I'm free.* I opened my eyes and looked up into the face of the most enormous seagull I had ever seen.

"Uh... hello?" I wasn't sure what else to say. "Thank you for saving me."

The seagull squawked. "We can't save you," it said. "You have to save yourself."

"But..."

"We have chased away the fragments, for now, but they will return stronger than ever."

"How can I stop them?" I asked. It felt strange talking to a giant bird.

"We don't know the answers you seek, but we can take you to the one who does."

"Take me?"

"Climb onto my back," said the gull.

"Oh… okay?" I said. I pushed myself up from the ground, feeling better and stronger every second.

I climbed up onto the back of the gull and held onto his neck. We took off flying higher and higher into the air. Up above the sky was dark and looked like a normal sky, not the swirling purple of the Dreamrealm at all. *Where am I?* I wondered.

I could see a rectangle of light above us, getting bigger. We were moving towards it. As we got closer, I realised what it looked like: *a trapdoor...or a skylight? We are going to go through it!*

We flew up through the rectangle of light and out of what must be the Rooms of Mind. *That was where they trapped me*, I realised; *they scared me into taking the pills yesterday so they could trap me there.*

Butterflies fluttered in my stomach as we soared over the Dreamrealm, higher than I had ever been before. Snowy mountains stood in the distance, and a desert stretched out to the side. There was so much of the Dreamrealm I hadn't explored. We seemed to be flying towards the great lake that I had visited once before, with Veila. And I knew exactly who we were going to see.

# CHAPTER SEVENTEEN

"*H*onu!" I called out across the lake. I was exhausted, but I needed to make sure Veila and the Priestess Tree were safe. I waded out into the water, looking across its shimmering purple surface towards where I saw the 'island' last time. *Nothing.*

I swam out, through the shifting patterns of the lake's surface, recalling how fun it was to be here the first time, how light and playful that day was compared to now.

The surface of the water looked like liquid glass. There was no sign of the giant turtle.

*Where are you, Honu?* I was starting to panic. What if the only person who could help me wasn't here anymore?

*Down below, child.* I heard in the back of my mind. "He's here!" I said to myself. What a relief.

*Come up!* I said to Honu, in my mind; *I need you; we all need you.*

Bubbles appeared a few meters from where I was swimming, disrupting the lake's glimmering patterns, making them more and more complex, and the water began to stir. I held back, remembering how enormous Honu was.

Ripples rose and spread out across the glassy surface as the 'island' re-emerged, complete with plants and everything.

"Honu!" I called out, as I saw his head pop up from the water, just a few meters away. I moved closer and flung my arms over his head. "I'm so happy to see you!"

I started to tell him everything that had happened with the Politician and Judgement.

"I know, child." he said. "I have seen…"

"The gulls think you can help me," I said. "What should I do? I know they will come after me again, and I'm worried they might go after Veila and the Priestess Tree to try to get at me."

"They may as well, young Dreamweaver," said Honu, "but I cannot tell you what to do, only you can determine that."

*No! The only one who can help me either can't or won't.*

My mind raced with terrible thoughts.

"Please," I said to Honu. "Please help me; you're my only hope."

"I said I could not tell you what to do," said Honu. "But certainly, I can help you."

"How?" I asked.

"What is it you need to know more about?" Honu

asked. "What understanding will help you in your quest?"

I thought about it for a moment.

"All this stuff with Judgement and the Politician... it's something to do with what you told me before, isn't it?" I said. "It's something to do with the Shadow."

"Certainly," said Honu.

"I know the Shadow is bad, but Veila doesn't seem to think that evil exists..."

"Evil is a strange human concept," said Honu. "The very concept of 'evil' is part of the problem we face."

"What do you mean?"

"The Shadow formed through disconnection, and 'evil' is a disconnecting concept. It only feeds into the darkness."

"I don't understand," I said, "and I have no idea how this is going to help me rescue Veila and the Priestess Tree from the fragments."

"Let me show you something," Honu said. "Press your forehead to mine." He lowered himself further into the water so that I could more easily reach his forehead. I felt the cool leather of his skin on mine. It was quite relaxing, despite everything I had gone through that day. I closed my eyes... and woke up in my bed.

# CHAPTER EIGHTEEN

*O*bviously, I was even more exhausted after the attack. I didn't want to get out of bed. I was sick with worry about Veila and the Priestess Tree and the whole Dreamrealm, and I knew it was all my fault!

*I should never have followed the voices – should never have let them trick me into taking those stupid pills. I've messed everything up!*

I was so busy worrying that I had forgotten what had happened with Felicity. When it finally came flooding back, I groaned.

I didn't want to deal with that on top of everything I'd just gone through. I tried to stay home from school again. I just wanted to get back into my dreams, but Mum wouldn't let me. I tried to tell myself not to worry, that things would have calmed down, and everyone would have forgotten the stuff Felicity had written all over the mirror.

I was wrong.

As soon as I walked through the school gate, people were staring: some made "oooh" noises. I sighed and looked at my feet as I walked, trying to avoid them, trying not to pay attention to the tightness in my chest that felt like it might explode through my spine.

I caught a glimpse of something different. A piece of pink paper was blowing in the wind. I glanced up at it.

*No flipping way.*

It was me – and Evan; our faces in a heart, printed out on pink paper. *Felicity,* I gritted my teeth, *that must have been the picture she snapped of me the other day.*

I did not see that coming.

I looked up to see identical pink paper all over school. I wanted to turn around and go back home – to hide under the blankets in bed until Mum got home. I would tell her that this was it.

*I'm not going back. I'm done with this school.*

I started to turn around.

"Awa," a low voice called me. I looked back to see Mr Jasper. He was standing next to the Principal, Ms Norton. I had only ever talked to Ms Norton once when Mum had brought me to the school to enrol.

Ms Norton raised her hand and beaconed me over with her finger. She looked like she was about a hundred years old, especially with the expression on her face.

"Explain to me the meaning of these... flyers!" she said.

I couldn't speak. My breathing caught in my chest.

Everything went grey. It felt like a million years had passed, but it was probably less than a minute.

"Awa," Mr Jasper said, gently. "Let's go into Ms Norton's office. Come on."

I followed them.

I could hear the kids laughing and jeering, but the sounds around me were almost drowned out by my extremely loud heartbeat, thudding in my chest like a basketball, ready to bounce out of my ribcage.

I'd never been into the Principal's office before. It seemed to have a lot of books on the walls, and I would have paid more attention if it wasn't for the pain in my chest. I sat down. I tried to relax; I tried to breathe slowly like Dr Spancer had taught me – like Veila had taught me. I hoped she was going to be alright. I wished I could be back there in the Dreamrealm right then. *Where are those gulls now when I need them?!*

As we entered the Principal's office, I imagined the gulls swooping down into the school to rescue me. I pictured the looks on the faces of the kids and teachers. That made me laugh. Mr Jasper and Ms Norton looked at me, and I turned my laugh into a cough.

"Awa," Mr Jasper said as he sat down in the chair across from me. "We need you to tell us about the pink posters. How did this happen? Do you know?"

I sighed. "Felicity."

"Felicity Cromwell?" Ms Norton said, her voice rising. "Our student council president? Our top student?

My heart sank. They weren't even going to believe me.

Mr Jasper nodded. "I thought so."

"You *did*?" Ms Norton and I asked at the same time.

Mr Jasper turned towards the principal. "I've spoken to you about Felicity before, Margaret. She has shown some concerning behaviours."

I relaxed a bit in my chair – *at least someone believes me.*

"This is concerning, indeed," Ms Norton said. "Why would a top student do something so vulgar?"

"She's a bully," I said. "Ever since I started here, she's been horrible to me – and it's not just me. She's been bullying my friend Ella for years."

"We will need to call her in, and call the parents in too," Ms Norton said.

"My parents?" I asked, my chest was tightening again. *My parents have enough going on without having to deal with this!*

"Both sets of parents. Please sit in the waiting room outside my office, Awa," said Ms Norton. She turned to Mr Jasper. "Colin," she said. "Bring Felicity in here; I'd like to have a word."

I spent most of that morning waiting. I sat in the waiting room outside Ms Norton's office for what seemed like a week but was actually just a few hours. Felicity had gone into the Principal's office and given me a murderous look as she passed. About half an hour later, a blonde woman had come in, who I assumed was

Felicity's mother. A little while later, a blonde man arrived too; he seemed to be in a rush.

The three of them were taking a long time with Ms Norton, and I could only guess that it was worse in there than it was out in the waiting room where I just had the ticking clock to worry about. I tried to read the mystery novel I had in my school bag, but it was hard to focus. I wondered what was going on outside, with Ella, Evan and the rest of the school. I wondered if the pink paper was still up there, giving everyone more reason to tease us.

The door of the waiting room opened.

"Awa!" Mum and Dad were both there. They were both hugging me. They looked worried.

"What's going on?" Dad asked.

I tried to tell them about Felicity, about the posters, and the bullying. It all came out in a muddled rush.

"It started right from my first day here. She just had something against me for no reason. She asked me where I was from and started calling me a mongrel..." I said, watching Mum's lips tighten. I knew I wasn't explaining it well. "She's just really mean!" It sounded stupid, but I didn't know what else to say.

The door to Ms Norton's office opened, and she waved us in.

It was quite cramped in the room with Felicity, and me, and both our parents and Ms Norton and Mr Jasper.

Ms Norton began speaking, kind of just the usual stuff that principals and teachers say when they are mad – like about expectations and being disappointed and expecting a higher standard at this school. It was hard to pay attention, even though I wasn't the one who seemed to be in trouble.

"I expect you to apologise," Ms Norton said to Felicity.

"I'm sorry," Felicity said, but she didn't *really* sound sorry.

There was silence in the room for a little while, and then Ms Norton stood up from her desk.

"Wait, is that it?" Mum asked.

We all looked at her.

"Excuse me?" Ms Norton said.

"Is that all you are expecting her to do – to apologise like that, in this room?"

"Vivian," Dad said, putting his hand on Mum's shoulder. "It's okay."

"It's not okay," said Mum. "What our daughter has had to go through is not okay, and neither is that weak apology."

"I will discuss disciplinary measures with the teachers at the appropriate time, but rest assured Felicity will be subject to our usual detention process," Ms Norton said.

"I'm not talking about detention!" Mum said, her voice rising. "I'm talking about an apology."

"Which is what we've just heard!" Felicity's dad said. Her Mum looked at the ground.

"That's not good enough," said Mum.

"What would you have her do? Write a bloody

159

letter?" Felicity's dad asked. He rolled his eyes. "Honestly… some people…" he muttered under his breath.

"That is exactly the kind of superior attitude that causes this type of toxic behaviour in the first place," said Mum, her cheeks flushed like they always do when she's mad. "And no, I don't think writing a letter would help your daughter's behaviour."

Felicity's dad looked like he wanted to swear, but the effort of holding it back just contorted his face into a funny shape.

"It needs to be a public apology, in front of the whole school," Mum said.

"No, Mum!" I pleaded. *This has been embarrassing enough.*

"As the Principal, I am the one who decides these things," Ms Norton said.

"And *you* are the one who has allowed things to get so bad," Mum said, "– so yes, you are responsible for this public apology – both Felicity and you. And if you don't do this, you are condoning racism, and I will have to make a formal complaint to the school Board."

"Racism?" Ms Norton and Mr Jasper both asked, their mouths hung open in surprise.

"Tell them what you told me, Awa," Mum said. I was silent. The shame froze me to the spot, and I couldn't speak… and so Mum repeated what I had said earlier, adding in that this kind of behaviour had human rights implications (she is a lawyer after all).

Ms Norton's and Mr Jasper's expressions were very serious.

The silence seemed to stretch on forever.

Mum and Ms Norton just looked at each other, while the other parents tried not to look at each other. Mum wasn't going to give in, and I guess Ms Norton sensed that.

"Very well," she said, finally.

I watched as Ms Norton picked up the phone and said, "Hello, Margie? Yes, please announce to the students that they are to all gather in the courtyard as soon as the lunch bell rings." Ms Norton glanced at her watch. "Actually, that's in five minutes – I've changed my mind, just tell the teachers to usher their classes out there now."

I didn't even realise I had been holding my breath, but I must have been. I let out a huge sigh.

*Why does Mum have to be like this?* It was bad enough being teased about the posters, but this is a whole other level of hell!

There was nothing I could do or say.

We followed Ms Norton out to the courtyard. The whole school was there, looking curious. At least the pink paper had been taken down. The kids all started talking when we came out, murmuring, whispering, staring. I'm sure my face was bright red, even though everything around me looked grey.

Ms Norton cleared her throat.

*Silence.*

"It has come to my attention, that there has been some awful behaviour going on right under my nose at this school."

Ms Norton looked at Felicity, and then back out at the crowd of students.

"So, I've called this meeting with you all, to clarify a few things."

She glanced at my mother, who nodded.

"I will absolutely not tolerate bullying and teasing, and especially not racism, such as that which has occurred recently. Students are unquestionably obligated to treat each other with respect and kindness," she went on.

I tried to make myself small, to shrink behind my parents, but it was pretty obvious what all this was about.

"With that in mind, I have an apology to make," Ms Norton said, there were a few quiet gasps and other surprised sounds from the kids, as if they had never heard a teacher, let alone the Principal, apologise for anything before.

"It is my responsibility, as Principal, to keep you safe and I was not even aware of the extent of the bullying behaviour going on, so I'm sorry to you, Awa," she gestured at me and I tried to shrink even more. "And to all of you... but it is not my job alone to make this school a safe environment – we all have to do better," she said. "I would like you to take this home and think about it: how can we be kinder to each other?"

Then Ms Norton turned to Felicity and said, "Now, Felicity, it is your turn to apologise to Awa, and to the school."

Ms Norton put her hand on Felicity's shoulder and guided her to stand in front of everyone.

"I'm sorry," Felicity said, but she didn't really sound sorry. She sounded angry. "I'm sorry about everything I've done at this stupid school."

"Felicity," her dad warned.

Tears had started streaming down Felicity's cheeks.

"I'm sorry about the posters, *okay*?" she said, her voice cracking. "I'm sorry about the mean things I said to you." She looked at me, and then looked back at the crowd. "To a lot of you."

She was really crying by this point; her face was red, and her voice was slurred.

"I was just…" she looked around. "I was just trying to make things better, okay?"

Ms Norton looked at her quizzically.

Something about Felicity's words sounded oddly familiar. It was so similar to what Judgement and the Politician had said.

"Everything was under control until she came along," Felicity continued, gesturing towards me. "Everyone listened to me… but she never listened!"

She broke down into sobs and stepped towards her parents.

"Right then," said Ms Norton. "Our task is to listen better to each other. We are all important here, and we must value and respect each other, all of us." She gestured around. "And now you may have lunch."

I didn't stay at school for lunch. I left with my parents. We went out for pizza at Toni's. I didn't feel like talking much, not after everything that had happened. Mum and Dad looked worried.

"Awa," Mum said. "I know I put you on the spot in front of the whole school."

I buried my face in a slice of margherita.

"I'm sorry that was hard, honey," Mum said.

"Yeah, why did you insist on a public apology?" Dad asked her, in the tone he usually took when they argued. *I hate it when they fight.*

"Let me explain," Mum said. "It was public, the way Felicity bullied you, it was in front of lots of students, the awful things she did…"

"So?" Dad asked.

I sighed.

"So, public acts like that deserve a public apology," Mum said. "If it were all in private, she could just keep bullying you, and no one would call it out. There would be no accountability. Now everyone sees the consequences – no one wants to face the whole school like that."

*Tell me about it!*

"She could still keep bullying me," I said.

"She might," Mum said. "But don't you think it's less likely after this?"

"I don't know," I said, grabbing another slice of pizza. I was starving after all the drama.

"Your mother might have a point," Dad said. "That girl looked pretty upset. I don't think she will be trying anything any time soon."

"It *was* kind of satisfying," I admitted. "I've never

seen her like that. She's always so smug. I've never seen her lose control before."

I was still contemplating the easiest way to change schools on the way home, and then I remembered everything that was going on in the Dreamrealm. The drama of the day had totally distracted me for a while, but now, worrying about Veila and the Priestess Tree... I was so tired that I could barely even watch cat videos online. I turned off the screen and lay down in bed. My body felt light, floaty as if all the stress of earlier in the day had escaped, and now I was free, except that now I had to help my friends...

# CHAPTER NINETEEN

*I* was back in the lake, exactly where I had left it, my forehead still pressed against the giant turtle's. I closed my eyes again. I needed to see whatever it was he wanted to show me.

A giant crystal prism floated through space, glistening, and glinting rainbows. *So lovely*, but something moved in the distance. I was sure it was a star, a shooting star, and then I remembered shooting stars aren't stars at all; it was an asteroid coming towards us! There was nothing I could do, as the flaming rock got closer and closer. I watched as it smashed into the prism, shattering it into splinters – some light, some dark, some in-between.

*These are the fragments,* said Honu's voice in my head. *The Dreamweaver can learn to alchemize them.*

*I wish I knew what that meant!*

I opened my eyes. "The Priestess Tree showed me something similar," I said. "But I don't really get it."

"What you must realise, Dreamweaver," Honu said, "is that there is no good or evil here. There was a whole, and now it is broken, and each of those parts is not to blame for their shape... for how they turned out."

Honu's words reminded me of my life – *before the divorce, it was whole, and now it's broken, and nothing will bring all the pieces together again.*

"But *how* can I alchemize them?" I asked. "Everyone keeps saying I need to do it, but no one explains *how* to do it!"

"Let me show you what I know," Honu said, bowing his head down into the water. I pressed my forehead against his again. And saw a man with a beard – the last Dreamweaver, how he learnt to work with the fragments, to build their trust, and how, after many years spent working in the dark in what looked like caves underground he managed to do it; in a flash of light he alchemized a fragment, with a peaceful look on his face.

"Where did it go?" I asked.

"Back into the whole."

"The whole of what?"

"Rest, Dreamweaver," Honu said. "Rest now, on the shore, and process. See what you find when you relax your mind."

"I can't rest! I need to find Veila and make sure she is alright."

"I assure you, she is fine, for the time being," Honu

said. "Rest now, you will need your strength to protect her, and all of us."

I lay down on the sandy shore of the lake.

So many pieces were floating around in my head, trying to solve the puzzle of what was going on, and what I needed to do. I was worried about Veila, and what the Politician and Judgement might do to her to try to get at me, but I needed to focus.

*The fragments have been disconnected, splintered off... does that mean they want to be reconnected?*

I rolled onto my front and rested my head on the sand. *All of that has something to do with the Dreamrealm... the fragments landed here, or this world was created after the prism shattered... maybe it isn't a metaphor, after all... maybe this is their world, and we just visit it when we sleep... their broken world, just like our broken world... or maybe... maybe this world is all inside our heads, and the fragments are something to do with us.*

I remembered how I could recognise some of the fragments in some of the things I did: getting stuck, wanting to hold onto things... wanting to be special.

All that thinking did my head in. It was too much! I started to feel dizzy, lucky I was already lying down. I thought about the last Dreamweaver again.

*It takes years to learn how to alchemize fragments – even decades; the last Dreamweaver was an old man before he managed to do it.*

*Maybe I need to ask a different question... maybe I can't alchemize the fragments yet, but I can stop them from hurting anyone... I could trap them somehow.*

I breathed out a long, slow, deep breath, and an image floated up into my mind out of nowhere. It was Narcissus. Sitting by the pool of water, gazing at his own face, reflected back to him... Narcissus trapped by his own reflection. *Where did that come from?* I wondered, but then I noticed something similar about Narcissus and the fragments, *they are all obsessed! – obsessed with themselves or with stuff or with having things a certain way...* Then I realised exactly what it was I needed.

I ran back into the lake and swam out to where I could see Honu.

"I have an idea," I said to the giant turtle. "So the thing is, I don't have years to master dreamweaving – to learn to alchemize fragments. I need to protect my friends *now.*"

"What is your idea, Dreamweaver?" Honu asked me.

"I want to try to trap them, instead... what do you think would happen if I held up a mirror to the fragments?"

"A mirror?"

"Yes, like Narcissus in the legend, he was so obsessed with himself that he was trapped, looking at his own reflection. Do you know where to find a mirror in the Dreamrealm?"

"I see..." said Honu, and he was quiet for a long time. "I will see what I can find," Honu said, finally, and he sank back down into the depths of the lake.

It seemed to take ages.

169

I floated on the surface of the water and looked up at the swirling sky, in all its different shades of purple.

Thoughts swirled through my head: *If the fragments are part of the Dreamrealm and dreaming is all happening inside our heads, then is it possible that the fragments are also part of us... part of me.*

I did recognise all their patterns – like the parts of me I don't really like... *but Dreamrealm is real; it's not just in my imagination.*

*Come on, Honu!*

I was so worried about Veila and the Priestess Tree. I thought about Judgement and The Politician, and I kept checking in case they had found me. Their attack kept coming back to me – the stress and terror. *I really believed I was going to die,* I realised, *and I don't even know what happens if I die here. Would I still be alive in the waking world?*

I thought about Mum and Dad and my friends again. It was all too much emotion. I splashed the cool freshwater of the lake on my face, trying to wash away my worries.

Something was changing... I looked across the surface of the lake; ripples were forming into waves, and Honu was emerging again. As he moved closer, I could see something in his mouth... a mirror with a lavender coloured frame.

"You found one!" I said, practically jumping out of the water with excitement. I wondered what other treasures were buried at the bottom of the lake.

I retrieved the mirror from the giant turtle's mouth,

and held it up to the light; everything sparkled; rainbows reflected off the water droplets on the mirror. I looked into it and saw...

"Oh... wow!" I said. It was me, but I was older, stronger, more powerful. I was wearing a belt with bright gemstones set into the front of it. I was glowing, beautiful, and intense.

"Honu, what is this...?"

"I will let you work that out, Dreamweaver, but for now, you must go and test whether your plan works."

"Don't you think it will work?" I asked. "I don't want to be doing all this for nothing! I need to do something to protect us from those... those awful creatures!"

"I cannot predict the future," Honu said, "but if your idea came from your own intuition, it is always worth trying."

The giant turtle smiled. "You may not get the results you expect, but you will learn more, understand more, and that is the most important part."

# CHAPTER TWENTY

"Thank you, Honu," I said, I started to move back towards the shore.

"Remember, Dreamweaver," Honu called out, "you are not without support... Ask for help when you need it, and help will come."

I thought about this as I reached the shore. I didn't really have a plan. I could just fly all over the Dream-realm, looking for Veila, or looking for Judgement and The Politician, but that sounded hard and exhausting. I realised I was still tired from the attack, but I also knew I needed to act now!

I heard a shriek overhead. *A gull! The gulls could help me!*

The last time I had summoned the gulls, I had called out to them in my mind, so I closed my eyes and focused on centring. *Gulls, wonderful gigantic gulls! I need your help; please come to the lake!*

I looked up to see the gull, that had been flying

overhead, turn and come towards me. It was joined by a whole flock of other enormous seagulls. They landed close by on the sand.

"What is it that you need?" the largest gull asked.

"I need to find Veila, to make sure she is okay, and I need to find Judgement and The Politician, to stop them from hurting anyone else."

"We will help you," the largest gull said and crouched down so that I could climb up onto his back again.

I clutched the mirror and held on tight as we flew up, higher and higher, over the Dreamrealm. The gulls spread out, scouting for Veila and my attackers.

The view from up there was sensational as always. If I hadn't been looking out down below, I would have been able to enjoy it.

It felt like we had been searching for hours, gliding over the Dreamrealm, but it had probably only been minutes. Every second counted.

I heard the 'caw' sound as one of the gulls turned and flew back towards us, continuing to call out.

"We've found her," said the biggest gull. "Your friend Veila is tied to the Priestess Tree…"

After a moment, he added: "It's likely to be a trap."

"I know," I replied, "but I need to help her anyway."

The gulls flocked together again, and we all swooped down towards the Priestess Tree. I could see something around the tree, but I was too far away to make out what it was. As we neared it, a peculiar thing happened. There was a clinking noise as a gull in front of us bounced off something.

"What was that?" I asked. A couple more gulls reached the same place and also bounced back as if they'd collided with an invisible barrier.

We landed close-by and scouted it out.

A giant glass dome became visible, surrounding the Priestess Tree.

The gulls tapped on it and tried to crack it, but it remained in place.

"Only the Dreamweaver may enter," said a voice. It sounded like Judgement, but she was nowhere in sight.

"This is certainly a trap, Dreamweaver," said the largest gull.

"I know," I said, in a tremble of terror. *They are so powerful*, I realised, *and no one will be able to help me this time.*

I just wanted to wake up, to get away from this whole mess, but I knew I had to go on.

I approached the giant glass dome, carrying the mirror.

"Put down your weapon," Judgement's voice sounded all around me, "and you may enter."

"This?" I said, looking down. "Oh, this is not a weapon," I lied. "This is a gift for you."

"A… gift?" the voice said.

"Yes," I continued, my heart pounding so hard in my chest that I thought it might jump right out. "It's a gift because… I've realised you are right."

"What?"

"Yes… you are right; some things do need to change around here… I'm… umm… really looking forward to all the ballrooms and stuff… I didn't realise it before, but then I thought about it, and I saw that you were only trying to do what is in everyone's best interests, so… so… I brought you a gift."

There was a pause. I didn't think she was buying it. I continued to stand there in front of the glass dome.

"What is your gift?" Judgement asked; her voice was suspicious. I still couldn't see where she was, just the glass dome and the tree in the distance.

"It's a mirror," I said. "So that you can see how wonderful you are."

I tried to smile.

After another pause, I heard her clear her throat. "A mirr-roar?"

"Of course, the Politician's voice said, "I know all about those… very state-of-the-art, top-of-the-line, great technology."

"Oh, yes, of course… Very well…" she said, a door appeared on the side of the dome, "but leave it by the entrance and come empty-handed to the tree."

*Better than nothing.*

I walked towards the door, and it opened, letting me inside, then quickly closed behind me. I put the mirror on the ground, leaning it up against the side of the enormous glass dome. Is lavender frame glimmered in the light as the surface of the mirror seemed to swirl.

I turned and sped up towards the tree. Dark indigo

ropes, wrapped around it, and around Veila. Her light was fading in and out, growing dim; she looked up at me. "Awa," she said, her voice quiet and croaky. "It's a trap."

"I know," I said.

"You have to leave," said Veila.

"No, not without you... and not without the Priestess Tree being safe."

"Ha haha ha..." laughter echoed all around the dome; Judgement's voice, mingled with the Politician's and the sound of others... cackling laughter.

"Of course, it's a trap," said Judgement, stepping out from behind the Priestess Tree. "And now we have you."

I scrambled, trying to untie Veila from the indigo ropes. I looked up just as Judgement hurled a giant ball of energy at me. I was knocked to the ground.

"Quick!" Judgement Cried. "Get her while she's weak!" The fragments appeared, so many of them I could hardly count. I recognised the tiny 'special' one and the hoarder who could hardly move under a waddle of precious possessions. There were others too, with strange faces, blank eyes... they held me down.

"No!" I said. "You... I see through all of you!"

My mind was racing so fast that my words couldn't catch up.

"You're shadow particles.

"The Shadow!" said Judgement, beaming. "We are very close, yes."

"The Shadow is marvellous!" said the Politician. "So, so, so powerful…"

"Oh yes!" said Judgement. "The Shadow is the antidote to all this horrific mess!" She gestured out to the Dreamrealm as she spun around.

"This time…" said the Politician, "you won't be able to get away." He began to wheel that awful machine out again. "And no gulls will save you… no amount of presents will be able to convince us to set you free."

I struggled under the weight of the fragments; they pushed and pulled and lifted me up into a chair.

*Not this again.*

I tried to push against them with all my strength, but it was too hard – much harder than trying to move through jelly.

*No, no, no…*

It was all too much. I could hardly see through all the fragments surrounding me, holding me down, blocking me off from everything else. There was nothing I could do. I slumped forward in defeat. *They're going to put that horrible mask on me, and it will all be over…*

Just then, I heard Veila's voice sound in the back of my head. *Don't give up; you have more power than you know.*

"This time, you will give us your power, and we will put it to good use," the Politician said.

"I want to help you," I lied again. It was the only thing I could think of that might change the situation.

Judgement looked at me and narrowed her eyes.

"Why would you want to do that?" she asked.

"I told you," I said. "You have good ideas – I agree with you – you are right." I was basically just saying anything I could think of.

"We are right," said the Politician. "That's very true."

"She's playing with us!" Judgement said, slapping the side of his head. His mask bounced off, revealing the red eyes and green skin of the snake below. I shivered as they both approached me. The snake hissed and slithered forward, out of the Politician's head.

"No," I said, "really – just look at the magnificent gift I gave you. It will help you – it will give you superior powers… the best powers… abilities you can only imagine."

A look came over Judgement's face. The Politician, who had knelt down to retrieve his mask, froze.

"Powers?" he said. "I'll just go and… err… examine it."

"Get back, you fool! It's mine!" Judgment yelled and began running in the direction of the mirror.

"No!" Called the Politician, slapping his mask back on and running after her. "I saw it first!"

"Hold her!" Judgement called out to the fragments surrounding me, but it was too late. They had forgotten about me. They were all staring, fixated, in the direction of the mirror.

"Mine!" said the hoarder,

"No! No! It's mine – I'm special, all the special things belong to me!"

They pushed and shoved, tumbling over each other on the way down towards the mirror.

I would have laughed if it hadn't been such a stressful situation, but I was already up, back at the tree, loosening the ties around Veila.

"Veila!" I said.

"No – save yourself," she whispered.

The ropes finally fell away. She floated up, her light returning.

"But..." I turned around, expecting to see the fragments approaching again, expecting they would be bored with the mirror by now, that they would have worked out it was a trick.

Strangely, they were still clustered around it.

"I think my idea worked," I said.

"What idea?"

"I read about this guy in school called Narcissus, who got trapped by his own reflection... and the fragments are all so self-obsessed, I thought it might work for them too, so Honu helped me find a mirror..."

She looked at me with pure wonder. "Amazing!" she said, and threw her little arms around me, making my neck tingle.

"Is the Priestess Tree alright?" I asked. I put my hand up against the side of her and listened.

*I am older than the sea*, her voice echoed in my mind, *and I am fine.*

"Okay, good," I said. We looked over to the fragments. "But what do we do about them?" I asked. "And this dome...?"

Veila shrugged.

"We could leave it up," I said. "To protect her."

*I do not need your protection, Dreamweaver, and I am not prepared to become a caged creature.*

"Okay," I responded, "but how can we get rid of it?"

"You are *truly* more powerful than you know," Veila said. "Come!"

She led me down to the edge of the dome, careful not to get too close to the fragments in case we distracted them from the mirror.

I could hear them arguing.

"It most certainly is mine!"

"No, it's mine!"

I expected to see them holding the mirror – pulling and pushing and fighting over it, but they were all just standing, a few feet away, staring at it as if hypnotized by their own images.

"Look at how perfect I am!" Judgement said. "Stunning, immaculate, absolutely spectacular!"

"But look at how charming and handsome *I* am!" said the Politician.

"Let's leave them to it," Veila said.

We got to the side of the dome, a few meters away from where I had come in, and where the fragments still stood.

"The door is gone," I said. "We're trapped!"

My gut tightened as my mind raced with terrible thoughts.

"Don't be silly!" said Veila. "Whatever power they used to put up this dome, it came from you."

"From me?"

"Yes," Veila said. "They must have extracted it from you using that machine thing. They don't have this kind of power on their own."

"But how...?" I looked up at the massive glass dome, *how could this have come from me? I wondered, and how the hell can I get rid of it?*

"Try putting your hand on it," Veila said.

I put the palm of my hand up against the dome, a dull sound rang out around us, like a giant glass being tapped softly.

The dome felt cool under my hand, but I still had no idea what to do. I looked at Veila.

"Okay," she said. "Close your eyes, and listen."

I did what she told me to.

"What am I listening for?" I asked.

"Your intuition – what you know deep down to be true."

"All I know is… that I don't know anything!" I said.

"Shush," Veila said. "Listen."

I could hear the fragments squabbling a few meters away from us, the sound of gulls in the distance; underneath that was a humming sound which could have been coming from inside or from outside.

Behind all this, I heard a tiny whisper of thought inside my head.

*Shrink it*, it said.

"Shrink it," I said to Veila "that is what I heard."

"Shrink the dome?" Veila asked.

"But how?" I wondered. "It's huge!"

I opened my eyes again and looked up at the enormous glass ceiling above us, trying to think of a way to shrink the dome...

*Nothing.*

"Try imagining it shrinking in your mind – but centre yourself first, like you learned to do when you figured out how to come into the Grove."

I closed my eyes again and felt the surface of the dome under my hand. I pictured it, as it was, in my mind, and then I imagined it shrinking, shrinking in a way that it dissolved around the edges of the things that it touched so that nothing was hurt as it got smaller and smaller...

"Wow," Veila said softly, beside me.

I opened my eyes to see the edges of the dome glowing with violet light as it became smaller and smaller, leaving everything in its path untouched. I watched as the Priestess Tree emerged, free on the other side of the glass. I watched as the dome shrank until it was just a fraction of the size, just surrounding us and the fragments.

I looked over at them.

"Do you think we should... leave them in here?" I asked Veila.

"It wouldn't hurt," she said. "Until you have worked out how to alchemize them."

"Won't they need to eat?" I asked.

"Oh no, they just need sunlight and exercise," Veila said. "And they will get plenty of that just by standing out here, fighting over your mirror."

Veila smiled at me, and I smiled back.

"But now... we need to get out," she said.

I don't know how I knew to do this; I just did: I drew a door in the side of the dome, just large enough for us. My finger left a glowing line as it ran around the glass. The line opened into the perfect little glass door, and we walked out into the fresh air.

I closed the door behind us, put my hand on the dome again, and imagined it shrinking, just a little more, so that it surrounded the fragments, giving them enough room to struggle over the mirror without taking up too much space.

"That was... weird," I said, and immediately I woke up.

# CHAPTER TWENTY-ONE

*I* was feeling amazing, lying in my bed... so proud that I had figured out how to trap the fragments and shrink the dome... that was until I remembered everything that had happened at school. I was not looking forward to facing all of that. I wanted to hide under a rock, or maybe a giant dome... but Mum said I had to go.

"You know that saying, 'get back on the horse'?" Mum asked.

"No," I said. I looked at my soggy rice bubbles, squishing some to the side of the bowl with my spoon.

"Well, it's a common saying, and it means that when you fall off – or something goes wrong, you have to get back up and keep going, or it only gets harder."

"Not possible," I said. "It can't possibly get any harder."

"Oh honey," Mum said, putting her arms around my shoulders and squeezing. "I know it was a lot to take –

and I know I put you on the spot. I'm sorry for that," she said.

I didn't respond. I was still too angry.

"Are you going to eat those, or just play with them?" Mum asked.

"I'm not hungry," I replied.

"Awa, come on," Mum said. "You're going to thank me one day."

"I doubt that," I said. "After making me go up there in front of the whole school? Don't you know I have anxiety issues?!"

"I'm actually really proud of you."

"I didn't do anything," I said.

"You stood your ground, honey, and you told me what happened, and that's what's important – if no one speaks up, then the racism will just continue."

"It wasn't that bad,"

"Awa," Mum leaned down until she was at eye-level with me. "Racism is not just what you can see – it hurts us – it hurts lots of people, and it's everywhere. Whenever we see it, we have to do whatever we can to stop it."

"Whatever," I said, even though something in Mum's words sounded annoyingly like the truth.

I did let Mum drop me off to school, even though I was trying not to talk to her. I just didn't have the energy to walk.

As soon as I got to the gates and into the courtyard, I could tell something had changed. Everything felt different.

As I walked through, kids looked at me, but not in the judgmental way they did when I first arrived, or when they were teasing me; it was totally different – they were looking at me as if I was a superhero or something.

"Hey Awa," some of them said, some smiled, some waved.

I was starting to feel a bit suspicious that I was actually stuck in a dream in the Rooms of Mind because everything was so weird!

I got to class just as the bell rang. Ella smiled at me from across the room, but we had a maths test and didn't get a chance to talk until the morning break.

I sat down with Ella and Evan at our usual table.

"Oh my goodness!" Ella said. "Everyone is talking about how cool you are."

"What?" I asked.

"Yeah," said Evan. "Yesterday, with Felicity and Ms N. That was extreme! I've never seen anything like it."

I sighed. "It was my Mum's fault."

"Fault?" Ella said. "It was incredible. I've never seen Felicity apologise to anyone – ever!"

"I guess," I said, peeling my mandarin, and trying not to blush. "But why is everyone treating me like I'm some kind of god now?".

"The thing is," Evan said, "Felicity has ruled this

school since we first started. She's found a way to bully everyone..."

"Or make them her friend," Ella said.

"Felicity doesn't really have friends," Evan argued. "She has servants – people who obey her."

"So your Mum just forced Ms Norton to do all that?" Ella said.

"Yeah," I said. "It was so awkward!"

"It was spectacular!" Ella said. "Felicity's face! She even cried."

"Yeah," Evan said. "I even felt kind of sorry for her. I never thought I'd think that in a million years!"

"And now..." Ella said, "Everything has changed... you know what it's like? It's like in the Wizard of Oz, where the house falls down on the wicked witch, and all the munchkins celebrate."

"I don't understand how Felicity had so much power in the first place," I said.

"I guess she just knew how to take power," Ella said. "You know, take people's power away..."

I nodded, thinking of the fragments.

"What?" Evan said. "What are you thinking about, Awa? You had a strange look on your face.

"Nothing," I said, wondering if I would ever be able to tell them the truth. "But you're right, it does feel different now."

I smiled at my friends.

# CHAPTER TWENTY-TWO

*T*hat night I had barely closed my eyes when I heard the sound of running water and bird-song, and I knew I was back in the Grove. I looked around. Something had changed.

The stream was even wider than before, flowing faster, sparkling, and churning in dazzling colours and diamond patterns. I moved closer. The pool at the centre of the Grove was perfectly still, despite all the water flowing to in and from it.

The kawakawa shrub still glistened in front of me, reminding me that there was still a message here that I didn't understand... *maybe I need to ask Nannie or Aunty Rosetta... maybe they'll have some clue about what the ancestors are trying to teach me.*

I climbed onto a boulder by the pool and dipped my hands into the cool water. I cupped them together and brought them to my mouth to drink.

It was like a fresh mountain spring was running

down my throat, cool and refreshing, uplifting, and revitalising every part of me – every cell in my body.

*Wow.*

I took a deep breath, enjoying the refreshing feeling.

Something flashed in the corner of my eye. I looked down to see a shimmer of peachy colour glide through the pool and disappear. *What was that?*

"Veila?" I called, wondering if she was somehow in there.

"I'm here," Veila's voice sounded behind me. I turned to see she was glowing brighter than I'd ever seen her before.

"There was something in there!" I said. "Something peach-coloured. I thought it might be you."

Veila laughed.

"I'm right here," she said.

"But what was it, then?" I asked.

"You'll find out one day," she said, "but I'm here to take you to the Priestess Tree. She has a message for you."

I followed Veila out of the Grove, along the forest path. Her peachy-coloured light glowed on the leaves as we passed, making shimmering patterns. Light seemed to flow out from her like little waves and ribbons.

"I've never seen you glow so brightly," I said.

Veila turned and looked at me. "You seem brighter too."

I looked down, surprised to see I had legs this time,

my body was glowing slightly. "That's strange," I said. "It reminds me of the mirror – I looked so different in it. I wonder what it means."

"It is mysterious…" Veila said. "Something has changed. It's all part of the process."

"What process?" I asked.

"You are becoming a Dreamweaver, learning your own powers and limitations, understanding yourself."

As we walked, the forest path opened out into dazzling bright sunlight. We had reached the Meadow. It also seemed to glow with more light and colour than before. A bloom of pink jellyfish swam through the sky again, colliding with a cluster of giant bubbles, sending sparkles flickering out across the sky. The grass shone in more shades of green than I ever knew were possible.

*Maybe it's me; maybe I just see more than I could before.*

We continued moving over the rolling hills of the meadow. After a while, we could see her, the Priestess Tree, standing tall against the swirling purple sky.

We passed the glass dome; the fragments were still exactly as I had left them last time, standing in front of the mirror, pushing each-other aside to get a better look at themselves. They didn't even glance up as we walked past.

"Funny things," Veila said.

"It's strange to think I was so scared of them, not that long ago," I said, "and now they seem so… harmless."

"Harm is in the doing," Veila said, and I thought I might know what she meant.

We reached the Priestess Tree, and I spread out my arms to hug her, pressing my face against her cool bark.

*I'm sorry,* I said in my mind. Giant tears sprang up and ran down my cheeks, saturating me and falling into puddles at my feet. *I'm sorry I put you in that situation, you and Veila, and all the others, I'm so, so sorry.*

*Hush, child,* said the Priestess Tree. *Come down to see me.*

I closed my eyes and let my mind wander down the tree trunk, underground, to see the Priestess. She looked even more vibrant than before – beautiful. Her eyes were shining, green like emeralds.

*Thank you, said her voice in my mind, you have protected the Dreamrealm, and saved us from the fragments who sought to upset the balance for their own gain.*

Of course, I said in my mind. It didn't seem like I had any other options.

*You are brave, Dreamweaver.*

*Me?* I laughed, *brave? I don't think so.*

*And you are stronger than you know,* The Priestess continued.

Veila had said something like that too.

*I'm just me,* I said, *don't get the wrong idea.*

*There is much work to be done;* The Priestess continued, *let me show you.*

Her eyes opened, revealing their vivid green colour as the circle appeared in front of her belly like it had the first time. This time I could tell it was a reflective disc, like a mirror, but it quickly began to swim with patterns.

I saw the chalice again – the one from my very first unusual dream… It was still a mystery to me. Then I saw the gulls – the same ones the Priestess Tree had shown me the first time we had met, only now the cryptic message made sense. *Of course, the gulls. They were part of the solution. They saved me…*

*The sea cliffs. Is that where the gulls live?* I wondered; *it's where Judgement and the Politician led me to the first time they tried to trap me.*

Merging into the sea cliffs, I saw what looked like the sedimentary layers of the earth, but it became clearer.

*Wow,* I gasped. *It's a maze!*

*A Labyrinth under the Dreamrealm,* The Priestess's voice said in my mind.

I felt tingles, spreading into waves of excitement at the challenge.

*How do I get there?*

*The sounds of your feelings will show you the way,* said the Priestess Tree, and I knew it was time to leave.

I followed Veila back across the meadow, towards the Grove.

"It sounds like you have a new challenge," Veila said.

I sighed. "Just when I thought things were going to get easy!"

"Easy is boring," said Veila, and we both laughed.

*The End*

If you enjoyed this book, you can pre-order *Into the Labyrinth: Dreamweavers Book 2.*

To hear all about the latest Dreamweavers updates, and get some cool giveaways, sign up to my mailing list!

# ABOUT THE AUTHOR

Isa Pearl Ritchie lives in Wellington, New Zealand. As a child, she loved creating imaginary worlds. She has completed a PhD on food sovereignty in Aotearoa. Her second novel, *Fishing for Māui*, was selected as one of the top books of 2018 in the New Zealand Listener and was a finalist in the NZ Booklovers Award for Best Adult Fiction Book 2019. *Awa and the Dreamrealm* is her first book for young people.

www.isaritchie.com

facebook.com/isapearlritchie

twitter.com/isapearlritchie

instagram.com/isapearlritchie

## ACKNOWLEDGMENTS

Many people have played an important part in the making of this book. Thanks to Jason Le Vaillant, Tesla Ritchie, Mandy Hager and Billy Moose, for all your advice and support. Also a big thanks to all the test readers who gave such excellent feedback: Mira, Giorgia, Vidthia, Maddie, Lachlan, Joy, Amélie, B, and a massive thank you to Tabby for all your help!

Made in the USA
Coppell, TX
12 February 2021

49301864R00121